NORTH

WILKERSON DYNASTY Book 2

KATHI S. BARTON

World Castle Publishing, LLC
Pensacola, Florida
Copyright © Kathi S. Barton 2020
Paperback ISBN: 9781951642990
eBook ISBN: 9781953271006
First Edition World Castle Publishing, LLC, July 20, 2020
http://www.worldcastlepublishing.com
Licensing Notes
Cover: Karen Fuller
Editor: Maxine Bringenberg

Chapter 1

North was ready to call it quits. Moving around the house he hadn't liked even before he walked through the front door, he decided he'd just live in the condo for his entire lifetime. It was better than trying to decide what sort of house he was going to buy.

"Sir, if you don't mind me saying so, you're going about this all wrong." He cocked a brow at Libby, the woman showing him the home. "Don't get me wrong. I'd love to sell you the biggest house on the market around here. But you're not thinking of this as a house to warm up to a home. You're looking for your home."

"There's a difference?" Libby smiled and told him there was a huge difference. "All right. I'm game for it. Tell me what it is I need to do to get myself done for the day."

Her laughter made him smile. He was glad that Abby had told him about this particular realtor. She was much like Abby, though older, and seemed to have taken him under her wing in an odd sort of way. Smiling again, he did as she asked and went out to the front porch with her.

"Close your eyes and think of this doorway you've just gone out of. Tell me what you remember." He looked at her. "Trust me. It's going to help you out with this. Tell me what you thought about when you first came up the steps to enter here."

"The door looks like it's from some kind of institution. The windows on either side of it are not right for a house this large. They look cheap and out of step somehow for the wooden doors." He looked at her. "I hate it. The door. It was the first thing I looked at, and it's soured the rest of the house for me. I guess you'd say the first impression was off."

"All right. That's good. Remember that the door and the windows can be changed by you. Now, what about the house? First impressions on it, and what you saw when you walked inside. You have to remember; the front of the house can be changed if you want to live here." He was liking this. North had no idea why, but it was helping him to see what his feelings were for the house rather than just hating it and not moving beyond that. They re-entered the house to the front entrance hall. "Now, the door is fixed. The glass on the side has been updated. What would you like to see in here that you didn't before?"

He didn't close his eyes this time, but looked around, changing things as he went, such as the wallpaper in the room next to where he was. Then he changed the flooring.

His mind skittered over the staircase twice before he came back to it. That was the issue.

"The stairs are off-center. What I mean is, it looks like they've been put in as an afterthought. I suppose I could change them too, but then the room would look off balance because of the way everything is centered squarely around the staircase." She told him they'd move on to the next house. "This really is helping me. Thank you so much."

The next house was just as bad for him. As an attorney, he wanted balance in his home. North had never considered himself to be obsessive compulsive, but he did like things in straight lines where they were needed, and curves that would be well blended in the flow. Things just where they were supposed to be.

He was ready to call it a day, perhaps a week when they pulled up in front of the next house. Christ, it called to him. North got out of the car and stood staring at the way the house looked with the backdrop of the sky behind it.

"I saved this one for last because when you told me what you were looking for, that there should not be a long pretentious drive, I didn't think it would be something you'd like." Nodding at her, barely paying attention to what she was saying, he made his way to the front door. "This house had eleven bedrooms. Each of the bedrooms on this floor has a half bath inside. There is a shower/bathtub between each set of two bedrooms that would be shared. The master bedroom not only has its own bathroom, but it also has its own deck that has a two-person hot tub on it. Also, there is a place to bring firewood up to be used in this room."

"Are the turrets from the original build?" Libby told him that according to the paperwork, not only were the turrets built with the home, but there was extra shaped glass stored away in the basement of the utility building out back. "Several years ago, the entire house was sandblasted to remove all the paint from it. I have no idea why someone would have painted it, but it's better now."

There was a turret at each corner of the massive building, both front and back. He loved the way each of the three floors had a window looking out over the lands. How the very top of each of them had ivy growing from the top down. The way the house spread out from each of the sides showed him that someone had gone to a great deal of trouble to use a great many of the stones around the area. The walls between each window on the main floor were tall, stone, load-bearing walls. Going into the house, he decided that the front of the place just screamed at him to live here.

Libby laughed when he handed her back what he thought was the specs on the house.

"I'm sorry. Did I miss something? I've fallen in love with this house. I'm sure you know that without me telling you." Libby told him she could see that he had. "I'm not very good at poker either. Tell me this place isn't going to cost me more than the purchase price to have it brought up to this decade."

"The kitchen was redone just last year. The roofing gets a good power wash every other year. It's made wholly of slate with a tin seal under it. There is a new furnace and air conditioner on each floor. The house, only about ten years old, is about as modern as one could be, I've been told. There are no carpets in the home. I believe the homeowners didn't care for the way carpet had to be replaced every several years and opted to have area rugs put into the rooms. That way, they could change them out when the room needed to be redecorated." He asked her why the house was being sold. "The previous owner designed the house himself. You'll find large pieces of furniture in some of the rooms that cannot be removed without tearing out walls. As soon as the house was finished and set to be moved into, the man died. Not here, I assure you, but when he was visiting his parents in another country. That's all I know about that."

Nodding, she unlocked the door for him. Stepping in first, he turned to Libby and told her he wanted to buy it. The house seemed to wrap around him and make him feel like he'd just found the perfect house. Nodding, she handed him the paperwork.

"I know you want it, but I'd like you to go through the house once. That way, if you get up on the third floor, you can change your mind." He asked her if there was something wrong with the third floor. "Not that I've been made aware of. But the house has been sitting for eight years now, the first two in probate, without a single person wanting to go through it after seeing the front of it. Also, the drive to the house. The driveway is longer than some people want to travel, I guess."

North had started to leave Libby in the largest dining room he'd ever been in when he asked her if he could bring in someone to be objective. Nodding, Libby told him to do whatever he needed to make sure he was making a good choice. North decided if he ever needed any kind of land, he was going to ask for Libby. He was even going to recommend her to his cousins.

Calling Mars to ask him if he could come by hooked him up with Abby. She said she had time, she was bored. Asking him if she'd be good as a stand-in for Mars, he readily agreed. Abby had become the go-to person, since Holly had been murdered, for just about everything they did. He couldn't have been more happy than to have her in his corner, as well as the rest of his cousins.

When she got there, he was in the kitchen. While he knew how to cook, due to Holly, Mars's mom, taking the time to show all of them how to make a few dishes to survive on, Abby had been expanding his skills.

"Holy shit, North. This is a fucking wonderful kitchen. You have to buy this for that alone." Libby was laughing when she showed him the other features of the kitchen. Such as a large pantry for extra storage, a huge freezer, as well as a restaurant size refrigerator that would be good to hold food for parties.

The three of them walked the rest of the house. There

were rooms that had large furniture in them, but he found that he loved them as well. The master suite had a bed in it that was larger than a queen in both length and width. It was the gas fireplace in the room that made him as happy as he'd ever been about a home.

"There are some things I am required by law to tell you. Nothing bad, but it does need to be disclosed. The bank has been trying to sell this home for several years now. Just recently, a company was set to purchase it, but there was a death in the family, and the deal was closed. In the back acreage of the lot is a family cemetery that—"

"What was the name of the company that was set to buy this house?" North wondered why Abby would care when Libby said she'd check. "Just wait a second, and I'll tell you why I care. It's important for all sorts of reasons."

"Abode Well." It took North a few seconds to catch up with Abby when she started to dance around the room. "Did I miss something?"

"Holly was going to buy it. If for no other reason than that, North, you must purchase this home." Abby looked around, then back at him. He was going to buy it, but knowing that Holly had approved in some way made it all the more special for him. "If you don't buy it, I certainly will."

He turned to Libby and told her he'd buy the house. "Also, you mentioned when we pulled in that there was an empty lot next to this one. I'll take that as well." Libby said there was a rental on that property that was currently being rented. "Who are they?"

"Mr. Oliver lives there. He used to teach here at the local school. He's retired now, and his wife passed on a few years ago. Lately, he's been late on his rent. That's something else I was going to tell you that you might have to deal with him sometime soon." North told her he'd deal with it later if that was all right. "It is. Once you purchase the house, all of that will no longer be a concern to anyone at the bank, nor my offices."

It took him nearly two hours to get to sign his name on the deed. With the help of Mars and his dad, he was able to get a very low-interest rate, as well as some extra from the equity from the house to fix the barn out back. It needed a new roof.

North took out a loan, even though he had enough money to pay cash for the house. His dad told him that the loan would help him establish a line of credit, as well as help the town. Always, he'd been told by Dad, help the town more than he had ever done. North, with his new outlook on life, told his dad he would do that.

Anything to help the town, after all, it had muscled through when his mom and aunts had gone on a rampage recently that ended not just in the death of his mother, but in all the other women being in jail. The five of them had done enough harm to the town and the people living here, North was still surprised the townspeople were nice to him and his cousins.

~*~

Amy had been summoned home from college a couple of times since she'd made a hasty exit. This time, however, had been different. She not only had her own place, but she was also making her own money. Not sure where to enter the house, she opted for where she knew she'd be welcome.

The timing couldn't have been better, she thought. While in town, she was supposed to look at some paintings for a person by the name of Wilkerson to evaluate them. Then she'd be in charge of cleaning them, bringing them back to their natural state. It was a hobby she did when she wasn't on a job taking pictures of animals.

Going to the back door of the house had been her way to escape all the drama in the front rooms. As soon as she walked into the big warm kitchen, Amy felt the stress of the last few days roll over her. The big hug from Lulu and her husband Hank was just what she needed. Sitting down when they asked her to, a large plate of not just her favorite fruits were given to her, but scones warm from the oven as well. A cup of tea, her preferred flavor, was also there.

Just like when she'd been living here, they never discussed the household, neither the people living in it nor her family. It was just the three of them enjoying a nice little break from whatever else was going on.

"I've been working out of the country since January. It's been fun having a new job waiting for me every time I finish one. Did you get the pictures I sent you?" Lulu told her how she'd been putting them in a big album. "I'm going to have the ones that weren't picked by the company I work for put into an album someday. They paid me for fifty pictures and ended up buying an additional fifty. I have no idea what they're going to do with that many shots. I've made it so they have to get approval from me for whatever they want to use them in. That way, they're not all over the Internet used as book covers. Not that I'd mind that, but I have to have some say over them."

"The one you took of the elephants playing in the water is my favorite of them all. And the monkeys throwing around leaves. They're all wonderful." She hugged Hank when he blushed brightly. "When are you leaving again? I'm sure someone is good as you isn't going to be idle for very long."

"No. I have two more shots this year for the same magazine, then I'm taking a month off. I don't have any idea what I'm going to do with so much free time, but I think I'll manage it." Lulu asked her if she enjoyed taking the water photos. "I did, as a matter of fact. The ones I was able to take of the polar bears was heartbreaking. They're having a rough time of it."

She turned when her dad walked into the room. He glanced at her, then looked at Lulu. "I'm sorry. I didn't know you had company." Then he looked at her again. "Amy? Is that you? My goodness, you're beautiful."

"Thanks, Dad." Unsure if she was supposed to hug him, she waited for him to make the first move. When he just kissed her on the cheek, she didn't let the disappointment hurt her too badly. "I had some extra time before I was to meet with you, then later the job I have. So I came to see what Lulu and Hank were up to."

"I can see that. Things have been very quiet around here." She figured with Phoenix gone on her honeymoon, things would be considerably quieter. Amy didn't ask about her or her mother but laughed when Dad asked for the same thing she was having—and was denied. "Just this one time, Lulu. You know how I've been keeping close to my diet."

He was eventually given two cookies and half a scone. Again, Amy didn't ask him what was going on. She'd learned the hard way that she wasn't a true part of this family. Phoenix and Mom had been louder and stronger than her since she figured out she wasn't welcome here.

Amy was never sure what she'd done other than to be born that had pissed them off. But since she didn't care much about parties and socially mandated appearances, she kept to herself and entertained herself when necessary.

"I've been meaning to get in touch with you for some time now. I wasn't even sure how to do that until I asked Hank. I'm glad you had them here for you, or I might not have been able to call you home." She nodded at her dad, wondering what she was going to be forced to do for a "family function" again. "If you don't mind, we can just talk in here. I've been confiding in these two much more than I think they wanted."

"No, sir. I'm just glad you finally got that big head of

yours out of your ass and saw what was going on right under your nose." Amy laughed at Hank. He'd always been one to say what he thought. It had helped her be what she was too. "Now, you go on and tell this little thing why you called her here. She's a right to know."

"Have you always been this pushy? If so, why am I only just now noticing it?" Hank told him he had that ass thing going on. Dad laughed, then looked at her. "I've filed for divorce from your mom. It'll be final in a few weeks. Phoenix isn't married either."

Amy wished she'd not been taking a sip of tea when he said that. It burned her lip and her nose as it spewed from her mouth. As she coughed her way to breathing again, she watched the rest of them try and mop up the mess she'd made while pumping her on the back to help her breathe. When she was finally able to inhale again, she looked at her dad.

"Phoenix isn't married? So Doug Schmidt is dead? I mean, that's the only reason I can think of that would make it so Phoenix didn't get her way. It would be death or— Oh no. She was caught with her panties down. Wasn't she?" Dad just nodded with a huge smile on his face. "Did Doug leave her at the altar? I do hope someone took pictures of it. That will do me— I'm sorry, Dad. I truly am. After spending all that money on her day, it was all for nothing. I'm really sorry."

"Only you would think of me in this. Thank you for that. But if I'm honest with you, and I plan to be from now on, I'd tell you it was well worth it. But Doug and his dad, they're thrilled so much that they paid me back in full for the wedding, as well as the tickets for the honeymoon. I'm not planning on telling your mother or sister. I'd like to let them think that I'm still out the money. It'll be good for them, I think. I guess the Schmidts were more thrilled that the wedding of the century didn't go on after finding out that not only was Phoenix a piece of trash, but she was an expensive piece too." Dad laughed, but even to her, it sounded bitter. "Fran, your mom, she was in the pictures I had taken of them with several of the groomsmen."

"You knew what was going on." Dad looked at Hank and Lulu. She did too. "You told him what was going on. Thank you for that. I don't care for Phoenix or Mom, but it must have been hard on you to have gone to Dad with this information."

"I hired a man to take the pictures. It was easy. The only issue I ran into was finding a night to pick from. Since the invitations went out, there had been an orgy of sorts going on here nightly." Hank handed her another scone, which she declined. "I didn't want another family hurt by them. What it came down to was them or us. We're too old to be cleaning up a room four times a day after the two of them had their friends over. Here, you've lost some weight you can ill afford, young lady. Eat."

"I have lost some weight, but I'm not worried about putting it back on, thanks. At least while I'm here." She winked at Lulu when she huffed at her. "I'm headed out again soon, so getting the weight on right now isn't a priority. I need to be able to get in and out of places, and being the size of one of the elephants I'm working with won't be a good thing."

"What do you do?" She looked at her dad. "I know so very little about you that I'm ashamed of myself. I don't even remember the last time you and I had a conversation. It's totally my fault, I'm aware of that. But I just realized there is no relationship between the two of us."

"It is your fault, but it's all water under the bridge now. I mean, it's much too late for us to have you come to my art exhibits, or any of the other million and one things I was in while living here, with Phoenix and Mom always taking up your time." Amy knew she'd hurt him, but it wasn't in her to be lovey-dovey with him anymore. "I'm a photographer. I've been one since I graduated from college a few years ago. In the event you tell me you don't remember paying for it, you didn't. I paid my way —"

"That's enough, Amy. You've proven your point quite well, I think." She looked at Hank when he spoke to her. "I know you're hurt, but there is no reason whatsoever for your father to be made a target. You know it isn't entirely his fault that you stayed away."

"What do you mean?" She just looked at the plate in front of her without answering her dad. "Amy? What's Hank talking about? Tell me, please, why you stayed away for so long. I'm begging you."

"The missus and your other daughter made her life a

living hell while here." Lulu took her hand into hers as she continued. "If she wasn't being ambushed and beaten by one or both of them while living here, it became a nightmare for Amy to even be in the same room with them. Several times I had to care for Amy when they poisoned her food. Food that I cooked, mind you. There were credit cards taken out in her name that she had to go to court over. Clothing of Amy's was torn to shreds, shoes filled with unspeakable things. Once there was a scorpion put in Amy's bed. If not for her spending the night in the hospital that night, she would have been killed, I think."

"Why wasn't I informed of any of this?" He looked at her, and Amy saw the exact moment he understood. "You did come to me, didn't you? You tried several times to tell me what was going on, and I shoved you away."

Dad stood up, and so did she. When he hugged her, then left the room, she sat back down. Not saying a word to either of the two people that had practically raised her when her mom and dad didn't, Amy got up and left the same way she'd come in.

Once she was in her car, she drove out the front drive and onto the main street. Once there, with nowhere to go, she decided to take a little time for herself. Finding herself a hotel with a pool, Amy opted for two nights and pulled her luggage from the trunk, full of clothing that was going to need to be washed before she could wear any of it. But instead of doing any of those things, she laid out on the bed and cried. Cried until her heart felt like it would never mend.

Waking when her phone rang, she didn't bother picking it up to see who it was. Instead, she staggered to the bathroom and turned on the water to take a bath. It had been literally years since she'd been able to soak in a tub.

The phone rang several more times while she lay there in the too-warm water. Amy tried to think of anything other than what was going on with her family for a while. Just as she was thinking there would be nothing to take her pain away, she remembered her good friend Booker Wilkerson. It only then occurred to her that he was more than likely related to whoever had asked for their paintings to be cleaned.

They'd been in a couple of classes together. Hitting it off as well as they did, they would go on shoots together during her assignments or when she was helping him study for this or that. Afterward, they'd go out to someplace fancy, always his treat as she was dead broke all the time, and then hang out at his place.

Unable to recall even a short conversation with him, Amy did wonder how welcome a call from her would be. Finding his phone number proved to be a tad more difficult than she thought it should have been. But once she found it, calling him was easy.

Getting a busy signal, Amy opted for not leaving a message. It was silly anyway, wanting to get in touch with someone from years ago. Putting her phone back on the nightstand, Amy pulled out her clothes to sort out. When her phone rang again, she saw the face of Booker. Wondering how much the man had changed over the years, she answered the phone with a smile.

"Amy Hamilton, how the fuck are you?" Amy laughed and cried as she told him she'd just gotten to town. "I'm going to pick you up, take you to dinner, then we'll go over all the shit that has happened since I spoke to you last. It's been far too long if you ask me."

"For me as well. I'm only home for a couple of days. I'm thinking I'm here to assess your family pictures. I'm staying in a hotel." After giving him the name of the place she was staying, he told her he was leaving now. He also told her that Mars, one of the cousins she never met, was the one with the paintings. "I'm going to talk to him soon, just not today. I spoke to my dad earlier today. I don't think I'm any more a family member than I was before. How is your family?"

"Too much to tell you over the phone. I'll be there in about ten minutes. I've missed you so much." Amy said she'd missed him too. Very much so. "All right, dear. You wait for me in the lobby, and I'll come in and get you. Remember what I've always told you, love."

"I remember. You told me that you are the only man in the world I needed. I don't know how true that is anymore. Do you?" He said he didn't know, but would be there soon. "I'll be in the lobby. I can't wait to see you."

When he came in the front doors of the hotel a few

minutes later, Amy went to him, sobbing about how much she'd missed him. As they hugged, talking over one another, she knew she'd made a good decision in calling him. If nothing else, she knew she'd feel better just hanging out with him for a while.

Chapter 2

North walked around the downtown house several times before he decided it was going to make a good place for him to have his new offices. His dad was walking around in another part of the home that would serve as both their offices soon. Dad asked him what he had in mind when he entered the room he was in.

"I love this place better than the last three. How about you? This place is homey and not too overdone. I think we'll have to have it redecorated, but other than that, it seems pretty sturdy." He didn't know shit about houses other than the information that Mars had given him yesterday on what to look for in a place he intended to buy. "I was thinking the furniture we intend to use should blend into this place rather than try and upstage the fact that we're wanting a place that isn't too sterile."

"I think a couple of pieces Mars is getting rid of might do until we find something else. Like that old desk of mine. I think I'd like to have that if the offer is still open for me to take what I want." North told his dad that Mars wasn't keeping any of the office furniture. "Good. I'll talk to him later about it. I'm all in for this place. I think we can do some good working from here. There is enough room that we can go about our day and not disturb one another too."

He and his dad were trying to get to know each other again. Since his mom was killed, North had been seeing his dad in a different light than he had before. The trial for the others, all his aunts, was being held soon, and he'd already decided not to have a thing to do with any of it. When his dad said his name, North smiled at him.

"You're all right with working with me here?" North said he was. "I'm still having trouble wrapping my mind around some of the things coming to light. I don't watch the news anymore either, as you suggested."

"I don't even subscribe to the newspaper anymore. I had no idea a paper could subsist on just one story. The fact that my mom was a horrific person seems to be breaking news daily." Dad nodded but didn't say anything. "Dad, we have to be honest with each other every time we talk about them. If not, we might as well just forget the entire thing about us making a new life with each other."

"I know. I understand that. But in my heart, I'm still having a hard time wondering when they'll stop finding more and more things she's done to people. Did I tell you Mars gave them permission to look around the back yard of the property? And the foundation under the swimming pool? Having found out about three people that disappeared while on the family land has taken a lot out of me." North told his dad it had him too. "On a better note, did you see how much work they've done on the kitchen? My goodness, having something redone in a place sure does make you realize how behind the times it really was."

Mars and Abby, two of the nicest people he knew, were living in a condo next to where he was currently living. He'd purchased a house, but it needed some work done on it, mostly painting and redoing some floors. Just yesterday he'd had dinner with them, and found out about the stash his mother had in her room to get away if need be. Each of the women in his family had the same thing—running money, they called it. Also, they found a list in each of their handwriting on things they'd done to people around the town. But the worst of it was what they'd done to Holly, Mars's mother, and Mars himself.

His mother and his aunts, all wives of brothers to Holly, had done some horrific things to the youngest Wilkerson. Holly had been kidnapped and raped over several days, and then when she was able to escape, the women talked the head of the family, North's grandfather, into turning her out. Mars then became a target of their hate, which drove a deep wedge between all the cousins and their fathers. North was trying his best to make headway into getting to know his father now. So, as far as he could see, were the other cousins and uncles.

"Your phone is ringing, North."

Pulling it out of his pocket, he answered with his last

name. He was taking a month off after quitting the firm he'd been working for, and was, so far, enjoying himself. Dad walked into the other part of the house as he listened to his cousin Booker on the other end.

"I'm having a little car trouble. Can you come and take me and an old friend to the restaurant?" North told him he could do that. "I'm sorry to have interrupted your office looking, but I've not seen Amy in a while, and I was really looking forward to this."

"I'll be there soon." Booker told him where he was. "Do you mind if we join you? You can say no, but Dad and I were going to grab some dinner anyway. I don't want to be a fifth wheel when you talk to your friend."

"That would be great. I told her so much about you when we were in college together that I'm sure she knows more about you than most." Booker laughed. "She's with me now—a great person. But I guess her home life wasn't all that great either. Her mother and sister were real bitches."

"Seems to be going around a lot. We found a building we're going to buy. I think it'll be perfect after we get it cleaned up and furniture in it." North told his dad where they were going, and they both headed out to his car. "I'll be there in about twenty minutes, Booker. I told you to get a new car, didn't I?"

"Yes, you did. But I can't seem to part with old George yet. He's gotten me through a lot of shit over the years. I was thinking about the times when he got me to Aunt

Holly's home when the weather was so bad. I'm surprised every time I think about it that I made it there in one piece."

It took them less time than he'd said to get to where Booker and his date were standing. The car, more than twenty years old, had taken its last breath, it seemed. Booker was waving goodbye to it as the tow truck took it away. Amy, the girl that Booker talked about all the time, shook hands with him and his father. Once they were in the car again, Dad rode up front with him and Booker and Amy in the back seat.

The restaurant was accommodating about adding two more chairs to the reservation. Once they were seated, North sat across from Amy. Dad and Booker were talking about new cars as Amy looked around the restaurant. Trying to bring her into the conversation, North asked her what she drove around.

"Motorbike when the weather is good. I have an old beater for when I'm home for more than a few days. I don't use much in the way of vehicles when I'm working." He asked her what she did. "I'm a photographer. I take pictures in the wild. Most recently, I was in the Amazon for a month. I have some nice pictures of the wildlife there."

They talked about what they did for a living until their orders were taken. Amy didn't say much. North didn't know her but thought she looked sad. That something had happened recently, and she wasn't over it. He looked at Booker when he started talking about the pictures Amy had taken a few months back.

"You should have seen them. Or you will see most of them, I guess. She was assigned to take pictures of an ant colony. You'd think that would be boring, but it wasn't. The way the pictures made you feel like you were a part of the colony could only come from her. I was telling her about Abby."

Dad asked Amy if she knew Abby. When she told him, no, she didn't, he told her about the wedding pictures she was supposed to have taken.

"What a small world. Phoenix is my sister, Fran, my mother. I was surprised as hell to find out when I got back here that there hadn't been a wedding." Dad looked at North like he was afraid he'd done something terrible by bringing it up. Amy must have noticed his look too. "It's all right, Mr. Wilkerson. I'm not close to my family at all. Phoenix didn't even want me at her wedding, much less to be a part of it. My mom is just as bad as, if not worse than, my sister. Dad is currently divorcing Fran, and I've not heard where my sister is living yet."

"She's currently living at a hotel with her mother." North asked his dad how he knew that. "I'm friends with Shelton, Amy's father. If she'd not mentioned Phoenix just now, I wouldn't have put them together. My goodness, your father must be thrilled to death to have them out of his hair."

"I guess he is. I don't know." North had a feeling they were zeroing in on what would be the topic of conversation she and Booker were going to have. "I was summoned home and found out that way. As I said, I don't have a great deal of closeness with my family anymore."

Salads were brought, and he noticed that Amy ate around her tomatoes. When he put out his plate for them, she didn't even hesitate and put them in his salad. As soon as he put his plate back in front of him to eat, his dad laughed.

"That's a first." North asked his dad what he meant. "You and a stranger sharing a salad like an old married couple. Are you sure you two don't know each other? Perhaps in another lifetime?"

Amy laughed. "I have no idea why I thought that was what he wanted. I can't stand tomatoes on a salad. Something about their texture makes me push them aside. But if they were grilled? Now that I could make a meal out of." North told her he'd never had them grilled. "Oh, they're so good with a thick steak. It's like a pop of sweetness with the meat. I also like them crumbled up on my omelets."

"I've known Amy for a very long time. Twenty years at least. She's also not a delicate eater." Dad asked Booker what he meant. "You know, North. The kind of woman you take out and regret her buying something on the menu because she isn't that hungry? Christ, I hate that kind of date. I want someone that orders what they want and eats the damned thing."

"He means me." Amy laughed again. "We went to a Mexican restaurant once, and I was able to handle the heat much better than he was. To this day, whenever I show up there, they look for the *sin calor americano*."

Dad laughed so hard he nearly knocked over his drink. North was able to speak Spanish too, but it took him longer to translate what Booker had been called than it had his dad.

"No heat American." Amy nodded at him while Dad teased Booker. "So I take it you enjoy your Mexican fare hot."

"I do. It's not worth eating if you can breathe around each bite. I love spicy food. Not so much in the way of sweets. I detest chocolate too." North laughed with her. "Once, when I was seeing this guy, he was forever buying me chocolate. No matter how many times I told him I didn't care for the treat, he'd buy it anyway. So one night, when he showed up at my door after a particularly loud argument, I took them into the kitchen and microwaved the entire box. Taking it back to the door, I slammed it in his face and tossed hot chocolate bombs at him until he got the hell out of my life. I think to this day, he still has a chocolate covered almond burn on his cheek."

Amy was delightful. Throughout their entire meal, she would tell something about herself or Booker that would have them all laughing. A couple of times, she'd mention her sister or mom, but mostly it was about the two of them becoming friends. Dad asked her how she'd met Booker. Booker laughed and told Dad he'd tell him later.

"Oh, now we all have to know. What did you do to

her?" Booker asked him how come he thought he'd done something to her. "Because I know you well enough to know you'd have to be the guilty one. If she'd done it to you, I also think she would have told us straight up without having to put it off until you were alone with us."

"I met him on a bus. We were going to this house, as a class, to see the classic design. It was a masterpiece. The most exciting thing about it was that it had been ordered completely from a Sears catalog. Every piece was marked as to where it was to go. There were even diagrams on the instructions." Booker laughed as she explained how she'd been off the bus first, while he'd been last. "When I'm standing back, looking at the house to get a good photo of it for later reference, Booker comes up behind me and lifts me right off the ground. I mean, he lifted me about three feet up. I took the picture, turned around, and kneed him in the groin."

Booker took over from there. "She makes it sound like it would have been a recoverable wound she hit me with. Christ, I couldn't piss for a week. I had to ice down my groin nightly so I could wear a pair of pants the next day. When someone tells you they felt it in the back of their throat, that is not just an expression. Amy can and will do that to you without a moment's notice. I've seen her use it on others too." Booker took her hand into his and kissed the back of it. "After that, we became good friends. She told me when I didn't retaliate, that made me the best as far as she was concerned."

"You two, are you dating?" Booker said no, and Amy said no way in hell. North asked them why not. "I mean, you seem to get along well enough. You even finish each other's sentences. Why are you so set on not dating?"

"We tried it once after I recovered from the kneeing. But it was all wrong." Dad asked him what he meant. "I don't know. But when the date was over, it was like kissing a sister or something like that. We're friends, not a couple. I know that makes very little sense, but it's never gone beyond the two of us just being what we are. Good friends that love to hang out together."

"Not to mention, he's afraid of me." Dad laughed with them, but North was studying the two of them. "Also, you'll not believe this, but neither of us drink, smoke, or do anything like other friends do. We're just good for each other."

North had no friends of the opposite sex. Nor did he have many friends that weren't related to him. No one that he could call on when he just wanted to talk something over. In that moment, he envied Booker and his relationship with Amy.

When dinner was over, Dad picked up the check. He said he'd not had this much fun in a long while and appreciated them letting him hang around with the younger crowd. Amy kissed his dad on the cheek and told him she enjoyed hanging around with him as well.

"I needed this. More than I can tell you." Dad hugged Amy and told her he did as well. "Thanks. I'll have to say my goodbyes here, however. I've decided to head back to work in the morning, and that means I have to find someplace to wash up my laundry."

She was gone before any of them could offer their home to do her laundry. Dad looked at North when they pulled up in front of the house they were going to buy. North waited for him to speak, as he'd noticed that Dad was a thinker before he spoke.

"Do you think they'll ever be more than friends?" North said it didn't look like it. "You should find her and ask her out, North. She's a nice girl, and I think the two of you could have some fun together too."

"What brought that on?" Dad said he didn't know, but he did notice how he'd been looking at her all night. "Looking and dating are two entirely different things, Dad. She's a beautiful woman, and I can and do appreciate that when I see it. Besides, I don't need an entanglement with a woman in my life right now."

"Entanglement or not, she'd be a good woman to have around when you need someone to lean on. Or not. What do I know? I married a bitch from hell." Dad was laughing when he got out of the car. When he leaned back in, he looked ready to cry again. "I could have done a lot better with my life had I found someone like her. I'm only saying that to have someone like her, not necessarily her, in your corner, son, it makes the bad things seem so much easier to cope with."

North found himself thinking about that all the way to

his condo. As soon as he arrived, he decided to call Booker and thank him for letting them join them for dinner. But what he ended up doing was asking for Amy's phone number so he could talk to her too.

~*~

Phoenix had seen Amy twice while she and her mom were in town today. Twice she'd tried to ignore her, and both times she wanted to run over to her and bash her head in. Not really, but it would have been fun to hurt her again. But there were three men around her all the time, and that just wouldn't do for her to get away with it. Phoenix was nothing if not cautious of getting her hands dirty when she didn't have to.

"Have you tried to call your dad today? You should tell him you're out of the rehab place and see if he wants to have dinner with you. For the sake of our family." Phoenix said she'd left him three messages. "Well, it'll do you no good to leave him any more. He's changed his number or something. I can't believe he did this to us. Left us with nothing more than a month's stay in this cheap hotel. Whatever gave him the idea he needed to have someone following us around taking pictures? I have to admit, I'm ashamed of how I looked in those photographs. Why didn't you tell me I'd put on some weight? I hate that I looked like your mother in those shots of us."

"Mother, are you even listening to yourself? You're complaining about how you looked in those pictures when that is what got us into trouble with Dad. What do we do to make him take us back?" Mom told her she'd been thinking on that, but her divorce decree had come today. "You mean he's actually going through with it? I thought you told me you had it in the bag. That you nearly had him saying how sorry he was that he'd not trusted you."

"I guess I overestimated my hold over him." Phoenix looked at her mother, and decided if she was going to ever get back in the house, she was going to have to do things on her own. "Besides, you don't know him like I do, Phoenix. Once he sets his mind to something, there is no budging him. But then he does have Amy around. Did I tell you I saw her at the house the other morning? Going in the back door like we trained her to do. I tell you, she was a great source of fun when she lived there."

"She never liked me. Did you know that?" Mom told her she'd not cared for her sister either. "Yes, that's true. I nearly had a stroke when Dad asked me to make a place for Amy to be at my wedding. Christ, why? When I asked him, he told me she was my sister and that family is all a person has. Whatever. She was never anything to me but a pain in the ass from the moment you brought her home from the hospital."

"I sort of enjoyed her as a baby. She didn't carry on very much. Not like you did. I think you were born spoiled. Amy didn't get into much trouble at school, either. At least nothing that I had to pay to get her out of. You cost me thousands." Phoenix told her mom she'd been born to party. "Yes, well, you certainly did enough of that in your last years of high school. Do you suppose Amy went on to college? She was certainly smart enough. But I never heard a thing about her after she left home."

While her mom talked about how precious Amy had been as a child, Phoenix tried to think of ways to get back to her life. Her dad had kicked her to the curb when he had Mom. Why, she didn't know. I mean, she was still his daughter. No one could dispute that. Wives were a dime a dozen. Children were forever.

"I wanted to let you know that the phones have been canceled as of today. I don't know if you tried to use yours or not, but mine is offline." Phoenix told her she only used it to take pictures. Thinking her dad would do something like shut off the phones, Phoenix was glad now that she'd written down the phone numbers she had stored in it. "Speaking of which, your wedding photos came today. Your dad must have had them forwarded here for you. I didn't open them, but I'm sure they're a mess. Did you ever find out who took the pictures of us at the house?"

"No. But I have an idea it was that cook. Lulu, of all names, must have told Dad about our afternoons. It's the only thing I can think could have happened. She was forever bitching about how much work we were creating for her by having guests over several times a day. The old biddy. I had no idea she knew what was going on up there until this."

Mom handed her the large envelope. Phoenix opened it and let the pictures slip out onto the table. "Those are all you got? My god. You'd think for as long as she was there, she could have gotten a few more pictures of me."

"Mom, it was supposed to be my wedding. Not you getting some photos of you." She looked at the pictures and realized not one of her bridesmaids had even called her after Dad had told them it was over. "I need to make a few calls. I'm sure that with me not living at home, Bitsy or any of my other close friends have not been able to contact me. It would be just like the staff to simply tell them I'm not at home anymore. I wondered why they've not made any attempt to call me."

"I'm going out in a little bit. Why don't you wait until then to call them?" Ignoring her mom in favor of doing what she wanted, Phoenix called Bitsy first from the phone in the hotel room. She was always a good friend when the chips were down. "What are you going to tell her about the wedding being off?"

Before she could tell her mom to hush, someone answered the phone. "I want you to get Bitsy on the phone now. Tell her it's Phoenix Hamilton." The man, whoever he was, cleared his throat. "Surely you can do that some other time, can't you? That's revolting. Put her on the phone before I tell her what a jerk you're being."

"Miss Bitsy has left strict orders not to put any calls from you through to her." She told him her name again. "Yes. I heard you the first time. She's not going to speak to you. We were told that if you were to call, we're to tell you to *fuck off*. Not my words, but hers, you see."

"You're lying." The man said he wasn't, and then hung up on her. "Mom, he hung up on me — the nerve of some people. I'm betting her parents are doing this. You just wait until I tell Bitsy what they said to me."

"Darling, there was that large article that told every detail of the scandal we were in. Her name was mentioned, as well as the other girls you know. Perhaps her parents are doing this to make sure she has a good marriage coming her way too." Mom laughed. "She'll need to be walking around with a brown paper bag over her head to have a man take a second look at her. Did you see how broken out her face was? My goodness. I was thinking then that she needed to be doing something before the wedding. That would have been a disaster."

That made Phoenix smile. But after calling the other girls she'd spent most of her childhood with, she found that they were not taking her calls either. Getting the numbers wasn't all that easy, either. Having to look them up in the phone book was difficult enough. Phoenix had to remember their addresses in order to make the correct call.

"This is just stupid. I don't know why they're all pissy with me. I didn't do any of this. Had Dad stayed out of it, as he usually did, I'd be on my honeymoon and living it up with Don." Mom reminded her that her husband to have been was Doug. "Whatever. It's not like I had any plans of staying married to him forever. He was just my test dummy like they use in those wrecking cars. Now I have no one to outlive and get all their money."

She'd been doing that a lot lately, just breaking down in tears at the strangest things. But she'd been thrown a curveball. Her life was nothing at all like it had been before. All her dresses were at the house. There was no one waiting on her all the time — cleaning up her messes, driving her around town. The most she'd been able to get from the house that day was a bag of her makeup, not even the good stuff. Just the stuff she wore when she was not expecting to go out or for anyone to come around.

"This is just mean." Mom agreed with her. "We have to make this right, Mom. I can't live like this. And what are we supposed to do when this month is over? I'm not going to get a job. I will not mess up my hands by doing anything menial. Dad has to see that he's ruining my life by having this little bit of a tiff with you."

"I don't think he's any happier with you, Phoenix. Nor do I think he cares at all if we have a job or not. Even our credit has been cut off." Mom shook her head as she looked around the hotel room they were sharing. "This is so below what I'd gotten used to by being married to Shelton. There has to be some kind of law that says he can't just dump us because of a silly affair."

"Silly or not, he's done a very good job of it if it is against the law." Phoenix looked out the window and saw Amy again. "There's that bitch now. Damn it. I wish I knew what the fuck she's doing back in town. I thought we made it perfectly clear that Dad and the two of us didn't want her around anymore."

"I thought so as well. However, as you can see, she listens as well as Shelton does. Do you suppose she's been given everything we had taken from us? That would really piss me off if she dared trying to use anything that belonged to me." Phoenix didn't point out that nothing her mom wore was anything anyone would want but opted for keeping the peace. She watched as Amy looked up and waved, then blew her kisses.

Jumping back from the window had her knocking the table over, along with the two chairs that had been brought in for them. The things on it rattled to the floor. The pictures that she'd been sent were spread out like a nightmarish rug, overlapping one another until she was nearly sick with the display. She noticed then that the shots from her bachelor party celebration were there, as well as a note from That Woman asking her to contact her if she wanted prints made of the pictures.

Screaming didn't make her feel any better, but it did startle her mom enough that she jumped back and fell too. Christ. Would this shit ever end? Phoenix decided right then and there that she was going to have a long talk with her dad and set the record straight, without her mom there. If she had to throw her mother under the bus, then so be it. It was war, and she wasn't going to lose this battle.

Going into the tiniest bathroom she'd ever been in, Phoenix fixed her makeup and hair. One of the things her dad could never ignore was how beautiful she was. Practicing a bit on how to look pitiful, Phoenix was ready to go. Getting there might have been a problem, but she knew how to get rides from people. Show a little cleavage, and she could have them eating out of her hand. Picking up her purse, she looked at her mom when she spoke.

"Where are you going?" Phoenix told her mom to mind her own business. "If you're going to see your father, I'm going with you. I want to get back home more than you do."

"I'm going to see him, but you're not going. I want to see if he'll take me back without you." Mom asked her what the hell she was talking about. "If only one of us is able to play him again, you know I'll be the one that wins in this. Once I'm in there, it'll be just a few days for me to bring you in too, don't you think?"

"I don't like it, but I think you might be right." Phoenix told her she was right. "You'd better not be saying this to keep me from going home too, darling. Remember, I know everything there is to know about you."

As she was going down in the elevator, Phoenix smiled. There wasn't any way she was going to be helping her mom out. If she got in, she knew she'd have her dad all to herself. And that suited her just fine.

Chapter 3

"You should come through the front door like family." Amy smiled at Lulu and told her she was working on the family part. "I'm sure you're not. Come in. And so you have a heads up, your dad has been coming in here every morning to have his breakfast. I don't think he's sat in the dining room once since this all started."

"I owe him an apology." Lulu told her she did. "Are you going to be nice to me? I got something for you the last time I was in Paris. Do you want it now, or do you want to bash me around a little more?"

"You need it at times." She did but handed over the large tin when Lulu sat down. "What did you get Hank? You always get us something from wherever you go. What's he — ? Oh, Amy. Oh, Amy, this is too much."

"No, it isn't. Here, let me help you get it open." Once she had the dark chocolate opened, Amy put several of the small chunks of it on Lulu's plate. "The lady that makes this is a good friend of mine now. I might have made her day by agreeing to take a bunch of photos of her granddaughter's birth. She's the cutest little thing. Anyway, I was there, so I also took pictures of the family gathered for the event. I'm rambling. So she asked me what it was I liked in the way of sweets. I told her I wasn't much into candy or things like that, but I had this wonderfully amazing cook that loved dark chocolate. She's mailed a box of them here for you."

"That's not necessary. You should have had her send you something." Amy explained to her that she owned a sweet shop. "Oh, well, then I will use this for you. Amy, this is wonderful."

Taking a taste of the dark rich treat, Lulu moaned. Amy had tried it and had decided right then that she was glad she didn't care for chocolate. It just didn't sit well with her on a great many levels. But mostly it was the bitter taste it left in her mouth when she was finished.

Her dad walked into the kitchen while Lulu was telling her about the hot cocoa she was going to make.

"You must try this, Shelton. I know you're not a big fan of sweets either, but this is divine." Dad took a small piece and moaned at the flavor too. "I'm going to make us both a cup of hot cocoa. I know it's warm out, but this will be a treat for us. Amy? What would you like to drink? I have tea if you wish."

"Tea will be fine." She glanced at her dad, then looked at him when he said her name. "I wanted to tell you I was sorry for the things I did and said to you. I was crude and cruel, and I'm sorry for it. My temper isn't all that stable when I'm feeling backed into a corner. Since I'd put myself in it, I should have been less bitchy to you."

"I wanted to tell you that I'm sorry as well. I've been a terrible father and a worse kind of person for the way I treated you. I'm not blaming your mother or Phoenix, but in dealing with them, I found it easier just to give in to their whiney ways." Amy told him it was all right. "No, it isn't. I should have put my foot down more, especially when it came to them getting their way. I'm profoundly sorry for that. I feel as if I lost a great deal more than I ever gained from the other two. I'd like for you—if you would, please—to move in here. I know your job takes you away at times. So if you'd use this house as your base, I'd love to have you around. To get to know you more than I deserve to."

By the time they finished having breakfast, they were on better terms. Amy had to stop herself a couple of times from telling him some of the things she'd been forced to endure living here as a child. But all in all, it was a wonderful way to start her day.

"I have a few things I need to wash up before I can move here." Lulu told her she'd do the washing. "I know how to do my laundry. You'd be surprised at how much I do for myself now."

"I'm betting you can. But I want to do this. You're my charge, no matter how old you are."

After accepting her offer of doing her laundry, Amy went out to her car to get her bags. She'd been planning to move in with Booker for a couple of days, but he'd understand if she decided to stay with her dad.

"Let me help you with that." Surprised or startled, she was still standing there with her mouth open when North took the oversized duffle away from her. "Anything else? It's not that far, so I should be able to take it in without dropping anything."

"I can do that." He turned and left her standing there. Reaching into the car, she pulled out her camera bags, as well as the tripod she'd had since she'd been sixteen. Once in the house, she saw North shaking hands with Dad and Lulu. "I met North and his dad yesterday when I went to see Booker. You remember him, don't you, Lulu?"

"I do. Nice young man. Despite having that witch of a mother." She eyed North a little before continuing. "I never cared for your mother, young man. She was a terrible person and not a good person to be around. I'm sorry if that isn't what you expected to hear."

"It's exactly what I feel, so I'm glad we're on the same page with that." He hugged Lulu, who seemed as shocked as she'd been when he showed up this morning. "My dad and I are trying to make amends. All of my cousins, with the exception of Mars, are dealing with a lot of horrific things our mothers were up to."

"Holly Wilkerson. She was your aunt." North's face brightened up at the mention of Holly. "Now, there was a wonderful person. When I fell a few years ago and broke my ankle, she rallied up some help for me, so this family was well cared for. I don't think anyone even noticed I was gone for nearly two months. Things went so well."

"I think I might have noticed you missing. It was in March three years ago, correct?" She nodded at her dad and smiled at him. "It was the corn cakes that tipped me off. They were good, don't get me wrong there, but they certainly weren't yours. Yours are so sweet and soft; it's almost a shame to put any kind of dressing on them."

"Oh, go on with you." Dad winked at her and North as Lulu sorted out her wash. "My goodness, child. Do they have stores where you're at? These clothes look like you're in threads. Why don't you buy you some more while you're home? Goodness. Look at this sweater."

Amy took the sweater from Lulu and held it to her chest. It was Dad who spoke next, her heart breaking with the words that spilled from his mouth in the telling of the origin of the sweater.

"That was my dad's sweater." Amy nodded. "He wore it most of the later part of his life, I think. I know he loved it. Amy got it for him when she turned sixteen. Every time I visited him, he'd tell me how she'd saved up her money and bought him the ugliest sweater ever made. I think that was another reason he treasured it so much. My mom hated it. So did Fran and Phoenix, now that I think on it."

"I asked him what he wanted that year. I had some money then working at the local photoshop. When he told me he wanted the most godawful sweater I could find, I thought he was joking. Until I saw this one hanging in the window at the local Good Will." Dad told her that he'd cherished it and her. "He left it to me, in his will. He told me that whenever I thought of him, I should hunt it down and put it on. It's worked for me every time I'm lonely."

For some reason she couldn't put her finger on when North pulled her into his arms; she clung to him, sobbing. It was a comforting hug, something she'd missed so much since her grandda had passed away.

When she collected herself, looking up at North, she thanked him for holding her upright. When he started to lower his head to hers, she backed away from him. Not sure where her feelings were at the moment, Amy took off to the front of the house. Anyplace to get her act together. Because kissing him, she thought, would be a total mistake.

"Are you all right?" She turned to look at North. He'd followed her? What kind of person did that? "Are you all right, Amy? I'm sorry if I took you off guard with holding you then wanting to kiss you, but— Actually, I have no excuse."

"Excuse me?" He laughed, and that tweaked her temper a little. "Listen here, buddy. If I had wanted a kiss from you, I would have taken it. I'm not some debutante that has to have a man on their arm, or they're not complete. You'll soon learn that I'm not just tits and ass. I'm a person who has a mind of her own."

"No, I can see that you're not some debutante. Nor are you all…what did you call it? Oh yes, tits and ass. You have a nice set of both of them, by the way. I did notice that you do have a brain as well. You'd have to have a good one to be as famous as you are." He took a step toward her, his face showing her how amused he was. "I looked you up last night when I got home. It took me a while to find out who you were. A. Jay Hamilton was as close as I could get to finding some of your amazing work. Why the name change?"

"Again, the tits and ass problem." She took a step back when he was only inches from her. "Why are you crowding me? I don't like to be backed into a corner, North. It makes me crazy, and I tend to say things I wouldn't normally say to someone."

"Never would I think you'd be a person that would be comfortable with being backed into anything. I'd very much like to kiss you. If you'd not mind." Her head was nodding, but in her heart, she was telling him no. "Thank goodness. I have no idea what I would have done if you'd said no."

The touch of his lips to hers was beautiful — not a word she would have normally used to describe a kiss. However, it was just a touch. When he did kiss her, holding her body to his, wrapping his arms around her tightly, Amy decided this man had had more than enough practice. It was almost like an art form.

His breath was sweet, minty almost. North's lips were tender yet strong, and when he used his tongue to open her mouth, Amy held onto him. The feeling of soaring through the sky, having rainbows dance along her spine, was too much and not nearly enough at the same time.

Then his tongue moved along hers, and her body exploded in sensations. Her skin tingled where he touched her. Amy was warmed by his breath, heated by his body, and when he rocked into her, his cock made her moan when he touched off something inside her that no one had ever touched before.

Tearing her mouth from his, she stood there in front of him with her head on his chest. His breaths were as rapid and as harsh as hers. Looking down his body, Amy could see the outline of his cock as it strained against the fabric of his jeans. North raised her chin up so she could look into his eyes.

"I didn't expect that." She nodded, not sure what to say to a man who'd awakened her entire being. "As much as I'd like to take this a few steps further, I think I'm rushing you along, and I don't want you to think that. I only meant for it to be a kiss. A way to taste you."

"I think you accomplished that. I mean, you were diving into my mouth like you were digging for gold." He laughed, and she smiled at him. "In the event you've not figured it out yet, I don't have a filter between my brain and mouth. By the time something spews from my mouth, my brain is too late in trying to clean it up. I'm a mess right now. Would you please take me out to dinner?"

"Yes." She asked him what he was agreeing to. "All of you. I was, I think, digging for something in your mouth. Perhaps the sassiness of you. The filter thing. I've noticed that as well. But I'm fine with that. I wish, as an attorney, I could be more like that with my clients. I'd love to take you out to dinner. But if we stand here much longer — this close, I mean — I'm going to try and figure out a way to see those famous ass and tits of yours."

She was giggling when he backed away from her. Amy couldn't remember any time in her life that she'd giggled. She supposed it was the way he'd made her feel — like a pretty girl with her first crush. Her dad cleared his throat when he entered the room.

"I wasn't snooping." North told him it was all right. They were getting to know each other. "I saw that. I'm sorry, but I overheard you were going to dinner together. I'd like for you to be careful, the two of you. Phoenix is on her way here. The people at the hotel are keeping tabs on them for me. I just wanted you two to be on the lookout for my soon to be ex-wife and my other daughter."

"Would you like it if I stayed here until she's gone, Mr. Hamilton? I have nothing else planned for the day if you need me." Dad looked so relieved at the question that he had to sit down. North went to him and asked him if he was all right. "If you're afraid of her, I can have one or two of my cousins come here too. Or you could sic Amy on her. I think she could handle her just fine."

"I'm not a child anymore. I think I can take her." She was playfully showing off her nonexistent bicep muscles. It had the desired effect, and her dad laughed. "What is she coming here for? I mean, did they give you a hint of her reasons?"

"No. Just that she asked the front desk if she could charge a limo service to bring her here. I've made sure the hotel is well aware of what I'm paying for while they're there. Nothing but the room. No extras." Amy thought that was too generous, but didn't comment. North seemed to know what she was thinking and winked at her. "If you'd not mind hanging around, simply for another person to hear her demands, I'd appreciate it. My biggest fear is that she'll hurt Amy."

"You don't have to worry about Amy, Mr. Hamilton. She'll never get to touch her while I'm around." North looked at her and seemed to have realized what he said. "I'm sure that Amy will agree with me that Phoenix has no power over her any longer."

It occurred to her that he'd meant more than he actually said about him taking care that she wasn't hurt. But almost as soon as she was ready to make him explain himself, the doorknob rattled like someone was trying to ensure it was in good working order. Amy said she'd get it.

Pulling open the door, Amy looked at her sister. It took Phoenix several seconds to remember who she was. It didn't make her any happier, Amy thought, for her to be in the house and she wasn't.

"What the hell are you doing here?" Amy said it was her home too. "Oh, so you remembered you lived here, did you? Don't get too comfortable, Amy. Mom and I will be back before you get too settled in. Where's Dad?"

She knew North had come up behind her because Phoenix sucked in her cheeks and puckered her lips. All Amy could think of was how much she looked like a dead salmon. Her cheeks and nose were so red from the walk here. Also, her hair had been blown around a little too much, and she could see her roots.

"Who are you?" The cat from Alice came to mind when Phoenix spoke. Amy started laughing before she could stop herself. North smiled at her, but she couldn't tell him where her thoughts had taken off to. "Amy, what the hell is wrong with you? Besides the usual. Get out of my way so I can come in and meet Daddy's new friend."

"He's my friend, not 'Daddy's.' Why do you call him that? *Daddy* makes you sound like you're six years old and need a long nap. I've heard you call him that when you're out together. I'm sure everyone in town knows you're pushing forty. Wait. You are forty. As of last month. Don't you think it's about time you called him Dad, like a grown up?" She could see she was pushing buttons on her sister. So when Dad came to the door, North took her hand and moved them both out of the way. "I was having fun." Amy put out her lower lip and felt stupid doing it.

"So was I when I was kissing you. But we can't have all the fun in one day." He kissed her on the nose before he turned to her dad. "Mr. Hamilton? Would you like for me to explain your rules to your daughter? Or have you done that already?"

~*~

Shelton watched the young man with his daughter. He liked North and thought he'd be good for Amy. But right now, he was dealing with Phoenix, and Shelton thought he was doing a bang up job of it too.

Amy moved into the living room, and he followed her. There were still things he wanted to talk to her about. Shelton knew today wasn't the day to do it, but he still sat on the couch opposite her. When the door shut in the front of the house, he wasn't surprised to hear the lock engage too.

"I was bluffing there, Mr. Hamilton. You do have a list of rules you gave them when you kicked them out of this home?" Shelton said he'd not thought of them, nor had his attorney mentioned them. "I'd tell him to get on that if I were you. I've told her a few of them you should demand that he have on the list—one of them being that they're no longer welcome in this house. Also, I'd add that they're no longer welcome on any property you own. At any point between now and when they figure out what I've done, they haven't any idea that they can move back into your home because you never set that rule for them. It's not a biggie. Most never think about it. But if they do, then you'll be screwed. Once they're inside, it'll be a bitch getting them out again. I'm assuming you've changed all the locks?"

"Yesterday, I had a man come out and do it." Shelton asked what else he'd have on the list. "In fact, I'm thinking I should hire you to take care of this for me. If you would.

Tayler is getting ready to retire, and it would be good for both of us to have someone there willing to take over for him."

"I've just quit my job in the city. I didn't care for working for a larger firm anymore. If you want me to run point on this, I can certainly help you out with things." North looked at Amy. "I'd like to see you on a personal level, Amy. So if you have any objections to me working with your dad on this, I won't."

Shelton looked at his daughter. It was, he'd bet, the first time she'd ever been rendered speechless. When she spoke, however, he knew this was her backed in a corner self. Someone he thought should be out more often.

"Why should I care if you're working for my dad? I mean, you're both grown men and should be able to— You'd have to be careful, I guess. Phoenix is— I mean, you shouldn't assume that you want to have a relationship with me yet." Her face turned a nice pink, she was so flustered. "You do whatever you want. I'm going to go in the kitchen and talk to Lulu."

She was mumbling something about men and their daft ideas. Shelton looked at North and could see the man was in awe of Amy. Also, he thought the boy was smitten with her. Laughing a little at the old word, North finally looked at him.

"She's a hellcat, isn't she?" Sadly, he told North, he didn't know her all that well. "I want to get to know her. Very much so. Anything and everything she'll share with me. I have no idea what it is that draws me to her — perhaps insanity — but I find myself aggravating her enough to see her temper show. Isn't that the stupidest thing you've ever heard?"

"No. I think it's funny, but not stupid. You like her, don't you?" North nodded and sat down across from him. "I'd like to ask you what your intentions for her are, but I don't think I have that right. We've not been on the best of terms. No, that's not right. We've not had an opportunity to know each other. That's my fault completely. However, if she'll allow it, I'd really like to get to know both her and you."

"She brings out the silliness in me. I don't know why, but it's been fun tangling with her off and on. Amy does speak her mind, doesn't she?" Shelton told him he'd noticed that as well. "All right, sir. I want to make a list of things you should talk to your attorney about. I'd not switch attorneys in the middle of whatever is going on here. Your wife could get in a few jabs I might not be aware of that was in any kind of contract you have with her. I'm assuming you had a prenup signed?"

"Yes. There wouldn't have been a wedding without it. She was pregnant with Phoenix when we married. I know that both the girls are mine. When they were born, I took care to find that out. I have several other contracts with Fran. One of them is that if she is caught having an affair by any means, then she isn't to get anything from the estate. Phoenix has something like that as well. Now that I think on it, I don't think I've ever given it to Amy. Not that it matters — I've not been responsible for her since she was six years old. My youngest is a very resourceful girl, I'm come to realize."

"I've noticed." Something moved by the window in front of the house. He asked North about it. "It's Phoenix. She said she wasn't leaving until she got to talk to you about this mess that her mom made. I'm not sure what mess she might be referring to, but I told her she'd have a very long wait."

Shelton told North all of it, even going so far as to tell him about Abby and her part in this. Showing him the pictures of his wife and daughter he'd had taken two days prior to the wedding, Shelton felt ashamed. He tried to explain what he was feeling to the younger man.

"I haven't loved my wife in a long time. It wasn't something I could have done anything about. Or I guess I told myself I couldn't. Her affairs were an issue, but since she never brought them home, or so I was told, I didn't worry about it. She knew to be discreet, I guess. But once I got the bill for the shopping trip for Phoenix's wedding dress, I started looking into other things. That was when I found out the shop owner had been asked to pad the bill for the dress so they could have some extra cash. Why? Well, I dug deeper into all sorts of things. Like how much I was forking over every month in the way of shopping sprees. You'd not believe me if I told you."

"My mother shopped. More like she demanded when

she went to find something. There were a group of them, my mother and four aunts. It's becoming clear to all of us cousins that our mothers never paid for anything they could bully their way to getting for free or just steal. Some of the things we're finding in her bedroom still have the tags on them. You've no idea how upsetting this has been for my dad." Shelton hadn't wanted to bring up North's mother. But now that he had, he felt he could ask him some things. He asked about the death of Holly. "Yes. They not only orchestrated the accident that took her life but also when she was kidnapped and raped over a few days. Lucky for all of us, Mars came out of it. Aunt Holly was more of a mom to all of us than our own mothers were."

"I'm so very sorry about that. I don't feel like I'm much different right now, other than not killing anyone. But I did neglect Amy. For that, I think I will feel guilty for the rest of my life." North didn't tell him he shouldn't feel guilty for what he'd done. Nor did he agree with him. Shelton, for some reason, thought it was just what he needed. A way to vent without someone adding more onto his already overloaded shoulders. "You'll stay for dinner, won't you? I don't have any idea what we're having, but I'm positive it'll be good."

Amy joined them in the room, and North stood up. Another reason to like this boy—he was polite to a fault. Standing too, he kissed Amy on the cheek and told her to make North stay for dinner. Leaving them to it, he went to the kitchen and asked Lulu if she minded having North stay. He should have done that before asking him, he thought.

"I'm already making plans for that to happen." He thanked her and Lulu turned to look at him. She had that serious talk look on her face, and he felt himself stiffening for whatever she told him. Lulu had been the one to call things like she saw them. Shelton figured that was where Amy had gotten it from. "I don't know if you're aware of this or not, but you're different since you got yourself shed of those other two. I think a wee bit of it is having little Amy here. If I don't miss my bet, I'm thinking that Wilkerson man is going to be taking her away from you again. But they'll be back. I'm sure of it."

"I hope so. I like him." She told him she did as well. "Good. We're in agreement on that. Phoenix is outside on the front porch. I'd avoid that if I was you. Or not. It depends wholly on what you want to say to her."

When she took off her apron and picked up a sheet of paper off the counter, he figured this was going to be good. Following her through the house to the front door, he was glad to see Phoenix backing away from her.

Lulu was only about five foot six inches in stature, but she made up for her lack of height by her forceful nature. Shelton laughed when North and Amy joined them. He also noticed they were holding hands. This might turn out a great deal better than he'd thought it might—a son-in-law of worth as well as a happy daughter. Yes, Shelton thought. Things were looking much better.

Chapter 4

North caught himself whistling. He would stop doing it only to realize he was doing it again. When Abby said his name, he smiled at her. She popped him on the back of the head.

"What was that for?" She told him he was being sappy. No woman liked a sappy date. "How do you know my being sappy has anything to do with a woman? It might be something else."

"It's a woman. Who is she?" He told her it was Amy Hamilton. He also told Abby her professional name. "That sounds like— Holy shit, North. Are you really seeing A. Jay Hamilton? Do you have any idea how famous she is? I mean, I have so many of her articles that— Have you seen any of her work? I mean, personally? I'd love to meet her someday. Why don't you have her over to dinner? She's the one that is coming here to do the paintings too. I can't believe I didn't put that together."

"You know her family." Abby said she'd remember if

she met her family. "I'm sure you remember her. Her sister is none other than Phoenix Hamilton. You do remember her and her mother, don't you? I think you called her BH for a while after you got home."

"You're dating someone related to Phoenix? There is no way I can believe that. Unless you're trying to pull my leg. Are you?" He said he'd never do that to her. She was dangerous. "I am. But really? Is she anything like her sister? I hope to God not. I'd hate to have to bar you from bringing her here for the holidays."

"I saw Phoenix today, so I can tell you with certainty that they're nothing alike. Amy's beautiful, smart too. In addition to being a famous photographer, she has a business management degree, as well as a pilot's license." Abby asked him why he wasn't with her right now. "I came home to get a few things finished up. I've been invited to dinner. And so I didn't make a total fool of myself, I decided to come here and calm myself down a little. I find that I want to spend all my time just staring at her. I might not have mentioned this, but I think she's scarier than you are when she's making a point."

"Good. I like her already. How much has she told you about her sister? I'm betting it was hell growing up with BH around." Abby was making bread, so her hands were occupied when her cell rang. Picking it up for her, he put it on speaker.

"Do you remember telling me about Phoenix Hamilton?" Abby told Mars she was just talking to North about her. "Hey, North. Anyway, she's been arrested for assaulting someone."

"Who? Amy?" Mars said he didn't know her name, but she'd been hit hard in the face with something. "Is she on her way to the hospital? I have to go there. In case... well, it doesn't matter which one of the women it is. I like them both."

His phone was ringing when he made his way out to his vehicle. It was Shelton. Answering as he started this truck, the older man told him to calm down and to take a breath, in and out. North asked him who had been hurt.

"Amy was injured, but not by Phoenix. She slipped, going back into the house to get Lulu's purse. Phoenix hit Lulu in the head with her handbag and knocked her against the house. Scared me nearly to death, I have to tell you. They're both fine, but I wanted to make sure they were so I called an ambulance." North laid his head on his steering wheel as Shelton continued. "Amy has an injury to her ankle. I don't think it's broken, but I don't have any idea. Lulu is going to need stitches. If I can talk her into staying the night there, I'd feel better. Would you join me here?"

"I'm on my way now." Putting his phone on the charger, his truck picked up the call and made it so North could talk and drive without being distracted by holding the phone. "I think my cousin is still on duty. I'll make sure he's had a look at them before he leaves the hospital. Wats is a great doctor."

"I'd be glad for it. I'm not even sure what happened. Lulu spoke to Phoenix before she left for the grocery store. I think you were leaving about then to go home. Remember?" He said he had pulled out after Lulu had. "Yes, that's right. A couple of hours later, I was going over the list that you gave me with my attorney when I heard screams. As soon as I got out to where Lulu was lying in her own blood, Phoenix was running toward the road laughing like a loon."

"How did Amy get hurt?" He said that might well have been his fault. "I doubt you caused her to hurt herself. She seems like she would hurt you if you tried."

"You have that right. But Lulu came around about the time Amy came down from the upper level and asked my daughter to get her purse. I told her it was in the kitchen, and Lulu told her it was in the car. When Amy turned to go in the other direction, she fell. I think she's more embarrassed than upset about it." North was feeling much better than when he'd left Abby. He could even start to see the humor in things. "I'm here now, North. They're not allowing me to go back until they have them examined. As you can probably hear, Amy is none too happy about having to undress and put on a gown."

"I'm pulling into the lot now, Mr. Hamilton." He asked him to please call him Shelton. "I can do that. I'd like that. I have to tell you, I've never been so panicky in my life as when I heard Mars tell me that someone at your house had been hurt by Phoenix. Abby, as I might have mentioned, is my cousin by marriage. She's married to Mars."

Shelton hugged him as soon as he was in the large ER department. Using his cousin Wats's name got him and Shelton back to see Amy and Lulu. He let Shelton hug her first, then he held her while she complained about how she was just fine. It was only a sprain. Wats joined them just as she was telling them she wanted to go home.

"It's broken, not sprained. And you'll do as I tell you or you'll be in a room all by yourself while I tell my cousin here what sorts of things you were calling me when I came to check you out. What a potty mouth you have." Amy stuck her tongue out at Wats. "Yes, that's very mature of you. I think I'm going to like you hanging around with us."

North looked at Amy when she asked him what he meant. "We hang out together. A great deal, as a matter of fact. Wats, along with the other cousins and I, were all we had for a long time growing up. I think we're closer than brothers." Wats agreed with him. "Mr. Hamilton—Shelton—I'd like for you to meet another one of my cousins. This is Watson Wilkerson."

After being introduced to the Hamiltons, Wats told them what had happened to Amy's ankle. He said she'd already had a small earlier break, and when she turned like she had, it rebroke the bone and did some serious damage to her ankle.

"Are you going to have to operate?" Wats told Amy he wasn't, but he'd assist. "I'm glad to have you there then. I don't do well under anesthetics. It's not too terribly serious, but I'm very difficult to get to come around. I think my body has an idea that when I'm down, I'm down for the count. I don't rest well, either."

"You'll have to stay off your leg for a few weeks, Amy. I'm sure you understand the issues that can arise from having a bone broken for the second time. I don't want you to have to walk with a limp if we can help it." She promised she'd follow his orders. "Good. Now, I'm going to go and see about Mrs. Martin. Mr. Hamilton, she was asking for you when she arrived."

When they were alone in the tiny cubical, North kissed Amy. He needed to know she was all right, and that helped tremendously. He not just needed it, but it was like he wasn't going to be able to breathe well until he was sure she was going to just fine. He sat down in the chair next to the bed, never letting go of her hand.

"You sure know how to keep a man on his toes." She looked ready to cry, and he got up and held her. "It's all right, honey. I was only joking."

"I know that. You're going to think I'm really stupid for saying this, but all I could think about when I fell was that I wanted you with me. I needed you to hold me. I've known you for all of ten minutes, it seems, and I find that I don't want to be anywhere but with you at my side." He pulled her chin up and looked at her. "I'm falling in love with you, North, and I don't think that is such a good idea. Not with all this shit going on in my life."

"It's the best news I've heard in all my life. I'm falling in love with you too. When I heard someone was hurt at your house, it was all I could do to get here fast enough to make sure you were all right. I know you can take care of yourself, but all I could think about was that I'd not been there to keep you safe." She nodded, and he sat back in the chair when she winced in pain. "I'm not going to leave you. I'm going to be with you every step of the way through this. All right? Besides, I have a family that is just as bad as, if not worse than, the one you have. We're a team in this."

They talked about themselves for the rest of the time they were waiting on her surgeon to show up. Once he did, telling them what was going to happen to her and how long she'd be in the operating room, Wats came in to ask if they had any questions. Amy asked if she was going to be able to be by herself.

"I'd rather you didn't. Not for at least a week. I'm not being pushy about anything, but I think your dad is going to have more than enough going on with Lulu and her husband. She's a handful, I think. Her husband, she told me, will be too upset to know heads from tails with her down. Is that about right?" Amy told Wats he was lost without his wife. "Yes, they're very much in love. Anyone can see that. So, not being pushy, but I'd feel better if you were to hang out with one of us after you leave here. I was thinking Booker could do the trick."

"No." They both looked at him, and North felt like he'd fallen into a trap that had been easily set up for him to fall into. "She can stay with me. I'll take very good care of her. How long will she be in the hospital? The house is without furniture right now. It's being painted, but the condo would probably be better anyway. It's all on one floor." Then he remembered who he was talking about. "That is if you'd like to come and stay with me."

"I wondered if I was going to have to remind you once again that I'm a grown fucking woman." He kissed her on the mouth. "Yes, I can stay with you. But no sex. I'm hurting, and when I jump your bones, sir, I want to be able to have as much fun as I possibly can."

Wats was still laughing as he left them to find out when they'd be taking her up to surgery. North asked her if she really wanted to jump him. When she nodded, he smiled. The meds the nurse had given her while Wats was there were starting to kick in.

"You're not anything I thought I'd ever want in my life. That didn't come out right, but I'm glad you found me." North told her he was thrilled as well. Holding her hand as her body relaxed and her eyes blinked closed longer and longer each time, he held her hand to his heart. "My head feels all woozy. I want you to be there when I wake up. Okay? I feel much better when you're with me. I don't know why. You're sort of a pain in the ass, but I'm in love with you."

"I love you, as well."

She closed her eyes for the final time then. He didn't leave her until he was told he'd have to go to the waiting room. The charge nurse told him Wats had made it so he could be with her in recovery, along with her father.

Feeling like he was on top of the world, North pulled out his phone and looked at things to put in his new home. However, just as he was ready to hit the buy button, he thought he should at least get Amy to approve of that sort of thing. North had no doubt that as soon as he could arrange it, the two of them would be living together.

Calling his dad, he told him what was going on. "You've found someone to love? My goodness, son. That's wonderful. Amy is a wonderful person too. I really enjoyed having dinner with you guys the other night. Have you told Booker?" He told him that since he and Amy were friends, she more than likely should do it. "He'll be happy for you. I know he will. Son, I have to tell you, these last few weeks have been like a new beginning for me. I feel like I'm able to start over, and it couldn't be better with you right here beside me."

"I'm glad you think that way, Dad. You, of all the people in this mess, deserve it the most." Dad told him all his brothers had been hoodwinked. "Yes, but you were married to the leader. I think that makes it the most difficult to get around. By the way, I've been meaning to ask you. Do you have any intentions of going to the trial? I'm not. I don't think any of the cousins are going."

"I was told I might have to testify on some of the things that came out after Eita was murdered. I don't know what I can add to what they found in her room. Mars would be better at telling them what was found. All I know about it is what he told me." North thought he might know a little more than his father did. "But I'm going to cooperate to the fullest. I've heard from the prison system again. Tina wants to see me, as does Penelope. I'm not sure what they think they can tell me that I care about."

"I don't either. If you want me to, I can go there and talk to them. All of them if you wish. I did tell them we were never going back there, but I think bothering you about shit is going to get them into trouble." Dad said he'd give it some thought. "Dad, don't do this if you don't want to. You don't owe any of them anything. They've made their beds, and now they are going to have to deal with what they've done."

"I know that too. I'm having dinner with my brothers tonight. We've been doing that weekly since Holly's funeral. My god, son. I missed so much about her." North didn't know what to say to his dad. He missed Holly more than he did his own mother. "On a cheerier note, I'm so glad that you and Amy are together. The thought of you happy does wonders for my depression. I've been battling it for a while now."

"It's more than likely what had me down for a while after she was gone. The thought of feeling nothing at all about the fact that my mother wasn't only dead, but that she was murdered. All I have to do is think of what she did to Holly over the years, and I want to go dig her up and make her pay." He looked at the desk when one of the nurses said his name. "I have to go, Dad. I'll let you know when Amy and Lulu are out of surgery."

Going up to the nurses' station, Milly, a long time friend of his, smiled at him. When he asked her how the surgery was going, Milly laughed.

"She's had to be given a little more juice. Wats called here to make sure that when you take her home, you strap her down any way you can. She's a pistol, he told me." North told her he was in love with her. "Well, of course, you are, North. It's right there on your face like it is Mars and his wife. Like having an electrical current running all over you. You make sure you keep her where she's supposed to be. We don't want anything to happen to any of you, Wilkersons."

"The ring." Milly asked him what he meant. "Aunt Holly gave me a ring. I completely forgot about it until this moment. I wish I could go home and get it for her."

"You have time. She's going to be another half hour or more in surgery. If they gave her more to put her out, then you might have an hour and a half to get home and get back." He thought for sure he could do it but was afraid of breaking a promise. "How about you call that dad of yours? I'm sure he'd be thrilled to no end in helping you out with this."

Kissing her on the cheek, he did just that. Dad was tickled to be able to help him. As soon as he sat down, the stress of the last few weeks — the renovations to his house, quitting his job, and anything else he'd been fretting over —

just slipped off his shoulders. It was the most wonderful feeling, he thought, to be stress free, if only for a few minutes.

~*~

Amy woke up and looked around the room. She was fuzzy on the details until she saw her leg up in some kind of harness. It didn't hurt right now, but she was sure if she made a sudden move or even wiggled her toes, she'd be in so much pain again, she'd be begging them for more drugs.

Dad was in the large recliner, snoring away. North was in the tiniest chair she'd ever seen. Then she realized it wasn't a tiny chair, but a very big man sitting in it. Turning her head at the sound of someone clearing their throat, she looked at the woman sitting there with papers spread out all over the table in front of her.

"What the hell is the difference between proprietor and owner?" Amy had to think a moment and told her she didn't know really, but they did sound like they should be the same. "That's what I thought too. But whoever wrote this thing is using them both to talk about the same person. Mainly Mars and I. I'm not an attorney either, but this thing is like unweaving a basket and trying to put it all back together again. Inside out. I don't know. I'd like to think I'm a tad bit smart, but this isn't helping."

"The word owner can apply to just about anything. However, proprietor is what the contract should be using. It's a business ownership. Why are you looking over contracts, Abby?" North kissed Amy on the cheek before taking her hand into his. "How you feeling? You've been out for a few hours. And I was thinking you were really going to be rested when you opened your pretty purple eyes."

"North, would you look this over for me? I've tried to make heads or tails out of this, but it's not written in any kind of straight forward contract like I've had before." North took the contract from Abby and looked at the first page before handing it back to her. "I don't know if you realize this or not, but there is more than just the front page in this sucker."

"This isn't from a lawyer's office. It looks to me like someone is trying to scam you." She asked him how he could tell. "There isn't a firm name on it. All it has is your name with your home address on it. I know for a fact you're not using your home address for your business. I helped you set up the P.O. box. Also, if anything, they should be sending this to the building you've opened in town. How did they think you were going to use your personal address for working?"

"It does mention something about our home here. The one that is being renovated, not the condo where we've been living." She found it and handed it back to North. Amy was sort of feeling left out, but the pain was making itself known to her, so she just let them do their thing. When North laughed, Amy looked at Abby. "What? What's going on?"

"It's telling you in a roundabout way that if they aren't happy with the photographs you take at their wedding, then they can take your business. Since they slyly put your home address on here, they're going to say you knew they were going to take your home along with the business when you signed this contract. Who wrote this?"

Abby told them the name she'd been given. Amy sat up a little too fast and asked them to hold on while she got her bearings again.

"I know them. I mean, not personally, but I've dealt with them before." She tried to think while the pain was taking over her mind. "I need something for pain. Now, please. I'll be able to think better. But don't sign anything that comes from them. Not even if it comes registered mail. They do this all the time. North, honey, knock me out, please, before I start screaming. This is fucking painful."

As soon as the nurse came in with a shot for her pain, Amy started to feel the effects of it almost as soon as the needle was taken out of the IV in her arm. While the pain wasn't completely gone, it was easier to deal with now that a large part of it had been taken away.

Her dad was awake now too. Just letting the magic of the pain meds take over, she answered questions from North and Abby about Highlander Weddings. North asked her if she did wedding pictures too.

"Yes. Just a couple of times when I was abroad and that was the payment for helping me track an animal. Mostly it was a few pictures of the bride and groom on the wedding day. Some with their family too. Not much. And nothing as good as Abby does." Abby thanked her, but asked how Highlanders had contacted her. "The same way, through a wedding they wanted me to take pictures of. I think I was in Africa then, taking pictures of some of the baby elephants. Could have been tigers, but that's not the issue here. I got a registered mail from them. It came via the post office I would use while there. I hadn't signed for it—one of the workers had."

"So, you contacted someone to see what was going on?" Amy told North she didn't have to. "Then how did you figure it out?"

"Ah, there is the question. I didn't. What I mean is, when the letter got to me, about a month after it was sent, Pat, one of the people helping me, said he'd seen the same kind of letter come to the office for others. Bad mojo, he told me." Amy remembered the look on Pat's face while he was trying his best to explain to her what the firm was. "After speaking to him about it, I sent it on to the company I was working for while I was there. They had more money than brains, and I let them deal with it. About three months later, I got a letter from the firm I worked for telling me I had nothing to worry about. I thought about telling him I rarely worried, but it was done, and I didn't have to deal with it."

Amy told them with how the contract was worded, Highlanders wouldn't have only been able to take her home if she had owned one, they'd take possession of all her work, including any future work if they weren't satisfied.

"How they'd get a photographer, in the end, was that they'd have some sucker take the pictures. The bride, they'd tell you, was unhappy with them. But since they really didn't want a house or whatever other things were listed, they'd cut the person a deal. One where not only would their firm get the entire set of pictures for free, they'd want the photographer to pay them an ungodly amount of money on top of it. A sort of win-win for them." Amy laughed. "I sometimes wondered if the wedded couple was even real. I mean, I could see them setting this up over and over. Can't you?"

"That's just terrible." Amy agreed with Abby but told her there were worse scams going on all the time. "What should I do about this?"

"Shred it. You win this round. However, you have to remember something. Even if Highlanders sends out a thousand contracts like this one and only two percent of the people fall for it, they're making a great deal of money all the time." Amy laid back on the bed and listened as Abby and North spoke.

Waking up, not realizing she'd fallen asleep again, she found North watching her this time from the chair. She asked him if she'd been out for very long. The pain was far more manageable than it had been before.

"No more than a couple of hours. They said if you wanted anything to eat, you should try something light.

But you can have some water. Not ice, because they don't want you to have the cold hitting your belly to quickly. How do you feel?" She told him not too bad. "Good. I need to tell you a good story. I'm saying it like that, so you don't think I'm going to disappoint you with some bad news. When Aunt Holly was murdered, she left some things in her will for all of us. Money and some other small things that all of us cherish as much as we did her. She also left us each a ring to use if we were to ever find someone to love." He handed her the box that it had come to him in.

"Oh, North. This is getting really serious here." He asked her if she wanted him to slow down. "No. I don't think I do. I'm in love with you, and I want to spend the rest of my life hanging around with you and your cousins." She asked him if there was a story with the ring.

"Yes. My great great grandfather bought it when he was Paris a very long time ago. He was a cheap bastard and thought he'd gotten a good deal by only paying ten bucks for it. Dad told me he loved Grandma dearly." Amy asked him what the real story was. "Well, Dad said that his great grannie took it to the jewelers and had the stone in it reset. It was then she was told it was nothing more than a shiny stone. However, this band was worth a small fortune. I've since had it appraised again, and the band is a treasure. Great great Grannie told my dad that the old buzzard, what she called her husband, should know better than to brag about how he'd gotten her something so cheap. If I remember correctly from my dad, when it was given to his sister Holly when she turned nine, it was worth just over a hundred thousand dollars. Grannie told Aunt Holly that she wanted someone in her lineage to use it to ask someone they loved to marry them. I gladly do with it as she wished by asking you, Amy Jay Hamilton, if you'd be my wife, forever and a day?"

"Yes. Yes, I'll marry you. Oh, North, I love you very much."

Kissing him was more touching this time. Like agreeing to marry him had with it a bonding magic that would see them happy for the rest of their lives.

Chapter 5

Bringing Amy home was a good deal more complicated than he thought it would be. Not only were there instructions on how to give her a shower, but how to keep her cast dry, how much she was able to leave her ankle lower than her heart. Which was, surprisingly for him, a thing that had to be done. But then, North was an attorney, not a doctor. Thankfully, they had one of those in the family.

"You have her pain meds and her dosage chart. You might have to keep reminding her not to let the pain get too far gone. When that happens, she'll suffer more, and neither of you are going to like that." North told Wats he didn't want her to suffer at all. "I know you don't, buddy. So keep an eye on her for us. I'll be over tomorrow, then whenever you might need me. I don't think you will, but don't allow her to take over her care, and I think she'll be fine. If she gives you a hard time, call Abby. She'll keep her in line."

For some reason, North didn't think having Abby come over would work. She and Amy were like two peas fighting over the same pod while laughing. He'd never seen anything like it. They were like friends and enemies at the same time. Sitting down on the edge of the bed that Wats helped him get for Amy, he asked her if she needed anything.

"Tired of me already?" He told her never going to happen. "Well, I'm bored out of my mind already. It's not you or this place, which I'm so glad you have, but I need something to occupy my mind. I can't get started on the paintings until the equipment I ordered gets here. That'll be time consuming, but it will be something to do."

"Would you like to help me with the case against your mom and sister?" Amy asked him what it was about. "Your dad has filed for divorce. And while I enjoyed talking to his attorney yesterday, I think he's a moron. Not on everything, but divorce isn't his cup of tea, I don't think."

"Probably not, I would guess. He's been working for my parents since before I was born. To be honest with you, I would have guessed he'd died a long time ago." North told her the man was nearly eighty years old. "That's about what I'd guess. I'd love to help. I don't know much about law, but I could probably look stuff up for you."

"I need someone to help me make a list of not just all the stores your mom and sister shopped from, but an accounting of how much was spent in a years' time. You can do it from a calendar year or wherever you want to start. Just as long as it equals a year with all the stores ending at the same time. Understand?" Amy said if she did January to December, then they all had to be the same year. "Perfect. This is a daunting job, I won't lie to you. I never realized two people could spend so much in a single store on a single day."

"I don't know what they did either. I'm to understand that Dad found several hundred thousand dollars in unworn clothing." North told her that was just in her mom's closet. "Christ. I'm betting because that was how she dressed when I was young, that they were all a decade or so too young for her. I don't understand why women want to dress like their kids. Sad, I think."

"I don't know. Some women, I think, can pull it off. They've aged beautifully and do look like their daughter's sister. But there are women, like your mother, that should look in the mirror before they leave the house." He handed her the first three stacks of stores. "I've separated it out by store name. At first, I was trying to put them in a date of purchase order. But like I said, there are just too many to cope with."

North made sure she had everything she needed to work with. He'd brought in a table to use while she was convalescing, and used that to his advantage. By the time he had an outline of what he was going to present to the judge, Amy had made some remarkable headway into getting the paperwork sorted by day of purchase.

"I was sure I was going to find a lot of return slips in

this mess." He asked Amy why she thought that. "I don't know, really. But I have read a few cases about women figuring they won't be married all that long and trying to build up a stash of money. To do it, they would buy things on credit. Then a few weeks later, bring it back for cash."

"That's what my mother was doing. I guess I never equated her having so much money to her stealing it from my dad. Well, perhaps stealing it isn't the correct word to use, but I think it was something along those lines." Amy told him it was stealing. "She didn't have a job, so I guess since she didn't contribute anything to the household, it might well have been considered that. Not only did my mom not work, there wasn't a household she had to run either. The nannies raised me. Then when I was old enough, I was cared for by the staff. I have a better relationship with them than I think is normal."

"Don't forget your aunt too. She did a great job making sure you guys were well taken care of. Look at this bill of sales. Why is there a tailored man's suit on here? My dad only bought his suits from Beckman's. He'd been going there for so long, they didn't even have to measure him much anymore." North took the receipt dated just three months ago. "If you look at the bottom, you can see where the man taking the measurements wrote it right on the bill. My dad isn't that slim. Nor is he that tall. It says the body frame is six foot six. Dad is, at best, six foot."

The more they dug into this divorce, the more things they were finding that Fran had done to make her life a lap of luxury while draining the bank account of her husband. Three hours later, North was still working on some of the things mentioned in the prenup that Fran had signed when she married Shelton all those years ago. Having made them both some sandwiches and brewed some more tea, he figured they were going to be there for another decade and still not be finished.

The knock at his door had him grumbling about visitors when he had a hurt bride in his home. Opening the door, he was surprised to see his uncles and his dad standing on his front stoop with smiles on their faces.

"We came to help you." He told them that wasn't necessary. "Well, we're all attorneys, North, and would enjoy this. Even though we're, for the most part, retired now, we still dabble in the law. Since this is your first case since leaving the firm, we figure you want to do a good job of sucking up to your future father-in-law."

Once he had given them all drinks, snacks if they wanted them, as well as a stack of paperwork, North carried Amy to the living room with his family. He introduced her to those she'd not met yet.

Taking his table in the room with them, North was sort of glad he'd not gotten around to buying too much in the way of furniture yet. There was plenty of room for them to have a seat on the floor and spread out their work. Not to mention, they all talked about their childhood, carefully not mentioning their ex-wives. It was wonderful to view a side of them he'd not seen before. And wouldn't have if his mother were still alive.

"North, there are several more bills here with men's suits on them. I don't see two measurements that are alike so far. She was spending Shelton's money to supply her lovers with clothing. That's a big no-no when it comes to divorces." North asked his uncle Aidan why, for his notes. "With just a rough estimate, I'd say there is well over ten grand here. I did read over most of the prenup he had her sign, and she's not authorized to pay for anyone else's clothing but her own or her children's. That's grand larceny. If she used a credit card, one that Shelton was paying off, to get hotel rooms for her fun, that could be a part of this too."

Uncle Wesley chimed in then. "I know you're doing this year thing for money spent on shopping and such, but with this kind of information, there won't have to be a payout for alimony. I know the prenup Fran signed says that Shelton can decide to pay her something over a few years if he wishes. But right here, as I would point out if I were trying this, would be more than enough for her to have been paid." North was making notes on all the things they were telling him. "How do you feel about what we've figured out for your dad, Amy? You think he'll go for it?"

"I do. I mean, I don't know him all that well. We're getting there, but for now, from what I've learned about him, I'd say he'd think this was about the funniest shit he'd ever heard." His family laughed too. "But seriously, I'm worried about Phoenix. She's going to point out that her name isn't on any of these receipts. Also, she didn't sign a prenup. I have a feeling she's really going to go beyond fucking him over."

"Is she over twenty-one?" Amy told his Uncle Wesley that she was nearing forty. "She still lives at home? And your dad still pays her bills? If I were your dad's attorney from the beginning, I would have advised him to kick her to the curb a long time ago. Also, I'm to understand there was a failed wedding. Something about orgies?"

"Yes. Abby knows more about that than I do, but there were pictures of both my sister and mom having fun with the groomsmen the day before the pictures were to be taken. Buck assed naked kind of fun." They laughed again. "Phoenix isn't a nice person. When I was living at home, I'd be a target for my mom and my sister every day. I was glad to leave home when I did."

"That sounds very familiar."

None of the uncles would look in his direction. They were all feeling the guilt of losing so many years with their sons and nephews.

Uncle Wesley cleared his throat and spoke again. "If you'd not mind, North, I'd like to stay here with your lovely bride to be while you're in court. I'm to understand it's the day after tomorrow."

"It is. Phoenix is in jail still, as her mom won't bail her out, so I know she'll be there. It's Fran I'm sort of worried about showing." Dad assured him she'd be there. "Why are you so sure? I'm not doubting that you're right, but why are you so sure?"

"If she doesn't show up, she'll lose out on making herself look like the victim in all this. I'd be prepared to hear a great deal about how Shelton mistreated her. Left her out in the cold at times. A whole slue of things that aren't true. Once you start telling the judge about her and her infidelities, it should wrap up easily."

"Do you think that will be the end of it?" All six of them laughed and said no way in hell. "Then what will happen after this? I mean, if I win a judgment in Shelton's favor?"

"All hell will break loose. Wear a vest to court." He said he didn't have one, then asked Dad if he thought it would be necessary. "If it's not, no biggy, but once you need it and you don't have it, then it's too late to put one on. I have one at home. I'll bring it over tomorrow. Abby has invited me to come over for dinner with you guys."

"What? Why are you so special?"

Dad told them he just was. The rest of them looked at North. "I think, for all the hard work we've put in for you, that Abby should feed us too. Don't you think so, son?"

He said he'd call her. Going into the bedroom, he was waiting for Abby to answer when he saw a movement outside his bedroom window. He knew who it was without having to check a second time. Just as he was going to the front to warn this family he thought it was Fran, Dad opened the front door.

~*~

"Where is he?" Clayton looked around the room, then back at her. "Tell me where he is, and I won't have to get into your shit."

"While that is a vision I'll never be able to get out of my mind, I don't even know who you are. Besides, there are a lot of 'he's' in this room, so you're going to have to narrow it down a bit more." She huffed at him, and Clayton laughed. "You're not a nice person. I'm positive you've been told that before. Haven't you?"

"My husband. Where the hell—? What the fuck are you doing here? Never mind. Don't answer that. I can see what's going on. All these men paying you well, Amy? I'm betting this is how you've made your money. Isn't it?" Clayton told Fran to shut up. "I'm sorry. What did you just say to me? I do not listen to people who are rude, you fucking shit hole."

"You sort of have a thing for shit, don't you? I mean, in the last few minutes you've mentioned it twice. Are you constipated or something? Or the opposite...you have the squirts? It could be, I suppose, something akin to texture or the smell. I'm betting it's the smell." Clayton laughed at the expression on her face. It was quite comical. Then he turned serious. "By the way, you talk to my future daughter-in-law like that again, and I'll bury you so deep in your favorite pile of shit you'll never get out of it.'

"Are you threatening me?" He said he wasn't. "That's good. Because my husband has a great deal of money, and he'll stop at nothing to get your ass into prison. He's very good at taking care of his family."

"Really? From what we've been working on all day, I'd say you're way wrong about that. It seems to me that Shelton is building a pretty solid case against you." North came up behind him. "This is my son, North. The one that is marrying your lovely daughter. The smart one, not the one that is currently in jail."

"How dare you." Clayton told her he was getting better at all kinds of things now—daring her was just something he thought she deserved. "You're going to regret this. See if you don't. If my husband were here, he'd take care of you."

"I sure would look forward to that, Fran. I'm betting he has a nice firm handshake. He'd be thanking me for telling you you're a fucking bitch." He shut the door before she could comment.

Looking at his family, Clayton was shocked to see them all staring at him like they'd never seen him before. Asking them what did he do, it was Josiah that spoke first. Amid his laughter, he explained what he was thinking.

"I think I'd like to hang out with you a lot more, Clayton. You've picked up some balls since all this began." He laughed harder. "I nearly pissed myself when you asked her if she had a thing for shit. Christ, I have to find a way to use that. I surely do."

The rest of the night was filled with laughter and fun. When his nephews showed up with food and Abby, he was amazed that in such a short time, not only had he gotten better acquainted with his son, but his brothers too. It was, to him, like an awakening. He'd been in a nightmare for so long, he was glad for every day he could spend with these men and women.

It was nearing midnight when he and the rest of his family decided to call it a night. He only lived across the street from North, but tonight it seemed such a long distance. Hugging each of his nephews, Clayton felt the pull at his heart. He'd missed so much. Not just hugs, but everything.

Holly, his baby sister, had been murdered. Before that, she'd been sold off to a bunch of men who brutally raped her. If that hadn't been enough, when she managed to escape, her entire family, including he and his dad, had turned on her, shutting her completely out of their lives as if she'd never been a part of it. All of it, every part of her life, had been because of the wives of him and his brothers. Clayton didn't think he'd ever be able to forgive any of them for what they did.

"Dad. She's coming." Turning, he saw a movement out the corner of his eye and moved forward enough that he was able to shove North out of the way, taking them both to the road, in turn saving himself from the speeding car. It narrowly missed them both. "Dad, she's coming back."

Getting up was harder than falling, he realized. Thankfully, Wats was close enough to drag his old ass up and between the cars parked in front of North's condo. He was still on the road but out of the way as the car sped by the lot of them. Clayton saw who the driver as she went screaming by them.

"That was Fran." No one moved as he laid his body back on the road to catch his breath. "She was going to kill us."

"I think she was after you." He looked at Brandon, who smiled back at him. "I just wanted to make sure you realize you might have pissed her off. I don't know, but it could be because you were into her shit."

No one moved for a ten-second count. Then it was like someone had touched a button and all dozen or so of them started laughing. Clayton was dismayed to see that in all the things going on poor Amy had made her way out onto the stoop. North went to her and put her back in the house while still laughing. Christ, it had been a hell of a night.

"I have to call the police." Clayton nodded at his nephew Brandon as he pulled out his cell. "I can't believe North saw her. If he'd been a second or two later…. You know what, I don't even want to think about it."

Neither did he, but Clayton knew it wouldn't be something he'd soon forget either. He'd been threatened before—being an attorney and a wealthy man married to a bitch, he got it a great deal. But to have someone actually try and kill him, and his son was something he'd never had happen to him before. He leaned against the car he was near and let things settle into his head. That was when he heard Amy yelling for him from the condo.

"Go to her, Dad. She's really upset." Clayton just

wanted to rest a minute, let his mind realize he'd not been killed. But he made his way to Amy to see what she wanted before he made his way home. He was going to wrap himself in a blanket and just sit on the couch.

"Are you all right?" He told Amy he was getting there. The slap to his face, then the hug, startled him somewhat. "While I'm enjoying the hug, would you mind telling me why you hit me first? I'm an old man, and I was nearly killed just now."

"That was for nearly getting yourself killed, you old buzzard. What the hell would I do without you? Answer me that. I just fell in love with your son and have you right there in my heart too, and you go and try to get yourself run over by a madwoman. Don't do that again, Clayton. It would break me in half to know you were hurt. Especially by my mom." She sobbed as she held him, and he wrapped her into his arms.

"I'm sorry I nearly got killed. I'm trying to work it out in my mind if you'd rather I did get murdered or not. You're not very clear when you're all mushy like this." She pulled back and looked at him. Her face was red, and tears streamed down her cheeks. "Oh, honey. I don't think in all my life anyone has ever cared enough about me to get all sloppy before. I love you, Amy."

"I love you too. I'm so sorry she tried to kill you." He said he wasn't dead, so they had that in their favor. "I can see now where North gets his sense of humor. It's an odd combination of smart assed and truth. I love it."

As he sat there, holding her hand while they were waiting on the police, every part of his body—and part of someone else's, from the way it felt—was beginning to protest the fall and the subsequent ass dragging across the road. There wasn't any way all this pain was just his. He had to be sharing with someone else. Wats came in with his little black bag, and Clayton told him he could give him everything he had.

"I hurt." Wats told him he thought he might. "I'm sure I'll be all right, but right now, I'd gladly take whatever you have on you just to ease it. Even just a little."

"You've cut your leg here, and I can see some blood on your shirt. Let's get you undressed so I can see what we're working with." He wasn't ashamed to remove his shirt. However, crying like a baby because it hurt so bad had him telling Amy and Wats how sorry he was. "It's all right, Uncle Clayton. I'm sure being able to save North was worth more than the pain."

"What?" Wats looked at him. "How did I save my son?" Wats told him he'd pushed him out of the way. That he'd thought Fran was after North, not him. "I only pushed him away so I could get us both out of the way of the woman. You really think she was after him?"

"That makes sense." He asked Amy why she thought so. "She would be more pissed off about me being happy than she would be someone just talking to her like you did. Mom was never happy until everyone around her was as miserable as she seemed to be all the time. Yes, I agree. She was after North."

By the time the police arrived, they'd all talked about how it had gone down. It did seem, upon reflection, that she'd been more going toward North than she had Clayton. The very telling part was that there were no skid marks prior to them jumping out of the way. Only afterward, when she turned around to make her way back to them.

"I'd like for you and North to go to the hospital." Clayton started to protest, saying that whatever was wrong, he was sure a little rest would help it. "Perhaps. But there should be a record of you having to be seen by a physician other than me for any kind of court appearance she might have to go to because of this. I'm sure you've thought of this, Uncle Clayton, but that was attempted murder just now. That's a biggy when it comes to having her put away."

"I guess you're right." He looked over at Amy. "Are you all right with this? Us taking action against your mother? I don't ever want there to be hard feelings between the two of us. I won't even press charges if you think it's a bad idea."

"You'd better press charges." He kissed her on the forehead. "Clayton, she meant to take you both away from me. Because as surely as I'm sitting here if anything had happened to North, neither one of us would have been able to cope."

"No, you're right on that. I've lost so much in my life. Mostly due to Eita. But I'm to blame as well. If I had lost my son, or you, my dear, I wouldn't have had the strength to go on. I don't think I want to think on that much." She told him she didn't either. "I'm going to press charges against your mother then. You just be safe too. Until she's caught, she is going to get more and more desperate to hurt someone for what she feels is an injustice to her. My wife was the same way."

"I'll be safe if you will be." Clayton told her he would. "When you get to the hospital, please make sure you two keep me updated. I can't go with you, and you have no idea how much that bums me out. Really, it pisses me off."

"I'll call you when I can. I'll have North do the same." She asked him why he was called North. "That's a story I hope you'll think is hilarious. Eita, for all her planning and scheming, could not spell worth crap. Her handwriting was just as bad. Asked to fill out the birth certificate, she put Roth as his middle name, but couldn't think of a first name. So she put N, for nothing, so she could go back and fill it in. There is no filling in later, she figured out. The certificate came back with North on it, and she never changed it. She didn't want anyone to think she was stupid and couldn't even spell her child's name correctly. Good thing for him he was born in a time where records people could think they were doing someone a favor and change names if they thought they were spelled wrong. Nowadays, however, he would have been 'Nothing Roth Wilkerson.' Try naming your son that someday and see what I mean."

The police took pictures of his wounds after asking questions. There were far more bloodied places than he'd first thought. Wats told him he'd meet him at the hospital, and left ahead of the ambulance. Since they were both up and moving, he and North rode there in the same one. He noticed that North was banged up as well.

"You need to marry that girl, son. Soon." He said he'd planned on surprising her tomorrow by doing it at the courthouse. "You don't want a large wedding? I would think with you both having professional careers, you'd want that."

"That is the reason we don't. It would be this large overly priced get together that neither of us would enjoy. I came back here to get away from all the noise and crowds. Not the only reason, but it had been my plan before Aunt Holly was killed." Clayton nodded, feeling just a little hurt by not being a part of his reasons. "After Mom was killed, I had no idea what sort of relationship you and I were going to have. Or even if we were going to have one. My plan to live here was to be nearer to my cousins. You've no idea how glad I am that you and I are making up for lost time, as well as getting to know each other again. Perhaps, I guess for the first time, we're having a good solid relationship."

"Thank you, son." North nodded, then pulled out his cell phone when it rang. After talking for several minutes, he put it away again. "Trouble?"

"They've arrested Fran. She was at the hotel. Not only did they get her for a hit and run, but apparently she didn't have a valid drivers' license either." North grinned. "She's telling them that I'm her attorney. I had to thankfully decline to represent her."

The two of them were still laughing when they pulled up in front of the emergency room entrance a few minutes later. Wats, true to his word, was right there waiting. As they were both taken to separate rooms, Clayton thought it would be a quick in and out. He couldn't have been more wrong. Wats had ordered a whole list of things to have checked, and he knew his son was getting the same treatment. Clayton could hear him bitching about it in the next cubical. This might not be so bad, after all. Not with his son entertaining him as he was.

Yes, Clayton thought, life certainly was a great deal more fun with his family around. He supposed it would get even better when the grandchildren came along. Christ, he thought, he could be a grandpa soon. Clayton couldn't wait. He was going to spoil them rotten. And there would be no one around to bitch at him for getting a little dirty with them either.

Chapter 6

North got home from the hospital just after ten in the morning. He was still sore and nursing a couple of sprains, but he was so happy to be there. Amy was in his bed, and he couldn't have been any happier about that.

"Hello, handsome." North grinned at her as he made his way deeper into the bedroom. "I made my way in here after everyone left. I thought about calling someone to come and help me, but it wasn't too bad. The only trouble I had was knowing which side you slept on. I took the middle."

"That's a good place to be." He took off his bloodied shirt. "My dad is going to have to spend the day at the hospital. We'd not realized he must have hit his head at some point. Wats found the wound on him when Dad complained about having a headache. He's going to be all right, but Wats wanted to make sure he didn't have anything more seriously wrong with him. How are you feeling?"

"Better now that you're home." He left on his boxers and climbed into the bed with her. It took them a few minutes to figure out a way for her to hold him without hurting until they finally settled down. "We sure do make a pair, don't we?"

"Yes. I was thinking that on the way home. Wats dropped me off with instructions for me to rest with you. I don't think that's his normal prescription when he sends people home. Do you?" Amy laid her head on his chest, careful of the several cuts on his side and ribs. "Dad was telling me that he hadn't noticed how badly he was banged up until he sat in here with you. He said it was difficult to maintain his manhood while talking to you."

"He cried like a baby. It was both sad and funny at the same time. He has a spot in my heart for saving you for me." North and Amy laughed. "I love that old man. Did he tell you I hit him?"

"Dad said you also hugged him, so to him, it balanced out. I love you, Amy." She kissed him over his heart, and he felt the warmth of it all the way to his toes. "I think this is the first time we've been really alone since I met you. Usually, there are a dozen people vying for our attention."

She had to get up to use the bathroom, and he helped her as best he could. It was iffy there for a few minutes when he sat her on the toilet. His nearly falling into the shower with her had him laughing so hard he almost fell on his ass. North realized he'd not laughed this much in all his life before she came into it.

The two of them were in bed again by noon. He gave Amy one of her pain pills — the almost spill had jarred her up a little. North took one of his too. Not that he couldn't handle the pain right now, but he thought if he wasn't fussing too much in his sleep about how uncomfortable he was, they both might rest better.

North woke to his cell phone ringing. The room was dark, and he was disoriented for a few seconds. It wasn't until Amy turned on the bedside lamp that everything came rushing back at him. Sitting up in the bed, careful of both their wounds, North asked the caller to repeat what he'd said.

"Are you all right, son?" He knew the man wasn't his father, so he told him he thought he was doing better. "It's your Uncle Hank. I was wondering if you wanted to have some support in the morning for this hearing. I know with all the information we've gathered, it should be a slam dunk for Shelton. I thought I'd see if we could offer you support in being there. For you and Amy. We all sure do like that girl."

"Yes, I'd love to have some support there. I have to be there at eight. I think the divorce decree is about eight-thirty. Then there will be a short question and answer session with Phoenix, Shelton's daughter." His uncle told him he had the itinerary in front of him. "Good. Amy isn't going to be able to go. She is still having some trouble getting around. I'm sore myself, but I think getting a night of good sleep has helped us both."

"I would imagine. I might have a way for Amy to join you in the courtroom. Remember a few years back when I went on a skiing trip with Penelope? I broke my leg. I hated skiing before—I positively loathed it after that. Anyway, I needed to get out of the house a bit each day, and someone in my firm knew a person— You don't care about that part. Anyway, I have this incredibly compact wheelchair that elevates a person's leg very well. Also, because it's so small, it's easy to get in and out of it if you need to." He asked his uncle to repeat what he'd said after putting the phone on speaker so Amy could hear. "I can bring it over today if you want to get used to it. I'm not very graceful, but I had no trouble at all getting it to work for me."

"I'd love that." She looked at North when she spoke again. "Would you and the other uncles mind if I called you uncle like North does? I really have taken your family to my heart, and I would love to sort of adopt you as my uncles too."

Hank was quiet for some time, so much so that North was afraid he'd hung up on them. But when he blew his nose and started talking, Amy held onto him as Uncle Hank spoke from his heart.

"Amy, you couldn't have made this old man feel any more wanted and loved than you did right there. For a very long time, I wasn't worthy of being called anything but bastard and asshole. Things have changed—I've changed. I'm even going to work on changing more. Yes, love, I would be very honored if you were to call me Uncle Hank.

I can also tell you the others would be very touched if you did the same for them." Uncle Hank blew his nose again. "Now, I have to get off here before I make a complete fool of myself. Well, more of one. I've cried a great deal over the last month. But this is, I'm thinking, the first time I've cried for joy. Thank you both for this."

He hung up before either of them could tell him goodbye. North looked at Amy and decided that asking her to marry him wasn't enough. He wanted her to know how very much he loved her.

"When all this started to peel apart, I had it in my head that I was never going to be a part of anything. Much less a loving family. Then I had a long talk with my dad, and we were, at best, working on a tentative relationship. The more time I spent with all of them—my uncles, my dad, and the other cousins—the more I realized that we were, for lack of a better term, fucked up." She told him she loved him. "And I love you too. I want to tell you that since I've met you, fallen in love with you, my life couldn't have been better. Even if you think about all the shit that has happened, you still love me enough to hold me in the middle of the night. To be a part of this family, one I thought I'd never want to be around again. I couldn't have done this, taken enough steps to be a part of my family again, without you by my side. Amy, there just aren't enough words in the world to even come close to telling you or showing you how very much I love you. And will for the rest of my life."

"I love you so very much too." They kissed again, and he laughed when his belly protested the fact that he'd not eaten in about twenty-four hours. "I'm thinking we should order us some dinner and laze around the house for a little while. You up for something to eat?"

"Yes." She went to her side of the bed and pulled open the drawer of the nightstand again. "Abby was here after you guys left—she came to bring me some things to keep me from being starved. You would have died laughing at me trying to carry a bag of apples and some bottled water while trying to get into bed." She handed him one of the apples and ate one too.

Getting up, he went to take a shower and thought of ways he could help Amy get one too. By the time he'd rigged up a chair in the stall and got her into the little room, he was ready for another nap. Just as he was pulling out his phone to order something, Mars and Abby showed up with big bags of what smelled like Chinese food. His belly growled so much he had a hard time covering it up and being made fun of.

While Abby helped Amy finish up with her shower, making sure she didn't slip or anything, he and Mars fixed up a makeshift table and chairs. Uncle Hank brought the wheelchair over but wouldn't stay for dinner. By the time Amy was refreshed as fuck, she said, they were all ready to eat.

They feasted. There was no other word for what they did when all the little white boxes and the tins of food were spread out on the table. They picked off each other plates. North tried things he'd never had before. Mars and Amy had a little competition going on—who liked their food the hottest. Of course, Amy won, beating Mars with three more shakes of hot sauce than he could stand.

"I was in Turkey a few years ago. I found this little place called *Plakasina Sicak*—Hot to Your Plate. They had the most wonderful dishes. They also had this hot bar. I have some of the sauces I bought in storage. I'll have to bring them home the next time I have to go there." Mars asked her how many languages she spoke. "I never thought about it before. I mean, I can speak a great many of them enough to get myself around. But fluently? I think about a dozen."

"That's amazing. I can speak Spanish and a little Cantonese. Mostly the later one so I could order when I went to the restaurant that was close to where I worked." Mars shook his head. "It's hard to believe I've been out of work for a month and don't miss a thing about it. I mean, I thought by now I'd be climbing the walls for something to keep me busy. But with all the businesses we've gotten and the other things we're trying to do to help others, it's like I'm busier now than I was working full time. But I do miss my mom."

They talked about Holly for a few minutes. It wasn't until Amy asked Mars how much he was worth that things got back to be silly. She seemed to understand it was painful for them to remember Holly.

"My worth is so huge I think it's a dream sometimes. My mom, she was one smart nurse. And a good money manager as well." Mars told her his worth. When she whistled, he winked at North. "How much are you worth, Amy? I know you've not taken a thing from your father in a while. He was telling me about that the other night. We looked you up on the Internet and didn't find anything until Abby told us what you called yourself when you're working. You have a very impressive portfolio."

"I've been very lucky in finding something I love to do and getting paid for it. And you're right. I've never taken anything from my parents. Not that I think I would have gotten anything, but I made my way in the world fairly easily." She grinned at him before she answered his question. "While we're not a multi-multi billionaire, North and I now have about three billion. I've invested well. Not on my own, but I've a good money management planner. We own properties in several countries that I frequent a lot. I've found it much easier to have my own digs while I'm working than to trust someone else with my equipment and darkroom."

North just stared at her. He hadn't known that. Not that it had ever come up, but he only assumed, wrongly as it turned out, that she was struggling. Amy certainly didn't act like someone that— Well, for that matter, neither did Mars. And he had a great deal more than anyone he knew.

"Are you upset?" North asked her why she'd think that. "I don't know. You have the strangest look on your face. Like you've swallowed a lemon or something. I didn't keep it from you. I just never thought to mention it. You have money, too, right?"

"I do. Not enough for us to live on for the rest of our lives, but I could put a dent in it. You said *we* own them. Are you saying you're going to keep me in a manner you're used to? I don't have a problem with it if that's your plan." She told him she would keep him no matter what amount was in their accounts. "Good. I can handle that. By the way, before the trial tomorrow, we're getting married at the courthouse. We were supposed to be getting married today, but…well, you know why we're not."

"Perfect. I was thinking it should be sooner rather than later. Perhaps we can have sex soon too." Mars spit water all the way across the room. It came from not just his mouth but his nose as well. Abby fussed at him about having the manners of a baby while she cleaned him up. "Abby, I think now would be a wonderful time to tell us something too."

"You mean about me having a baby? Well, I'm not so sure now. Just look at this big ape. Spitting out food like he's an infant. Though now that I think about it, do infants eat food? I don't know. But I guess there is no turning back—"

"What did you say?" Abby looked at Mars and asked him which time. "The part where you said you were having a baby."

"Why on earth would I have to repeat it if you heard?"

Abby looked at North. "Do you see what I have to put up with, North? He's forever doing this to me. Acting like a child. Making me repeat myself—"

"Abby Wilkerson." That shut her up. "Are you going to have us a child? Are you now pregnant with said child?"

"You make things so romantic, Mars. But yes, I'm about four weeks along. About the time we first had sex. I'll have to remember that in the future. You're potent." After they kissed, North asked her how she was feeling. "Really good, as a matter of fact. I've not seen a doctor as yet. I didn't know if Wats would want to take on delivering one of his cousins' children. It's sort of scary for me too. I've not had a great deal to do with small kids."

"Me either. I mean, I worked in a laboratory that was, for the most part, men. Not that there weren't women scientists, but I think my boss at the time, Chris Blevins, didn't have such a high opinion of women." Mars seemed to realize he was going to be a father. "Good Christ, we're having a baby."

~*~

Fran didn't understand a thing that was going on. Sure, she'd been caught by the police, but no one was dead, mores the pity. However, it was never her intention to kill anyone. She just wanted to rough up Amy's soon to be husband. Better yet, paralyzing him would have been so much better. But she'd not, so why was she still in jail? She was going to find out as soon as she got to the courthouse.

Another thing she didn't understand was why Phoenix

had to ride in a second van. No wonder their taxes were so high. Not that she had a clue what they were, but she would bet they were more than most people's in town. Mostly because she insisted that her home was the best. It never was, but she wanted that to happen someday.

They drove by the Wilkerson mansion on their way to the courthouse. There were trucks and vans parked all over the place, and she wondered about it. Asking the officer driving told her nothing. But then she noticed they were pulling out all the furniture and loading it into a van marked with *Billings Antiques* on the side of it.

"They're getting rid of the furniture? Why? I bet that place has more antiques in it than most of an entire town does." No comment from the front. When they stopped at the stop sign right in front of the old mansion, she could see into the house. "Christ, someone is taking the wallpaper down to the bare walls. What the hell is someone thinking with that shit?"

"Mr. Mars is moving in. After the death of his wife and the scandal with that, Mr. Clayton decided to give it to the rightful heir. Couldn't have gone to a nicer man, either." The other cop turned and looked at her. "You sort of remind me of Mrs. Eita Wilkerson. You two must be two peas from the same pod."

"That's the nicest thing anyone has ever said to me." The woman laughed and told her it wasn't meant to be a good thing. "Being compared to one of the nicest and most influential women in this town is a compliment in my book. Thank you for that."

The rest of the ride was done in silence. Fran had never taken the time to look around her little town. She noticed a lot of old buildings in disrepair—a lot of cars sitting in yards with grass growing up around them. One of them had a tree growing right out of the window in the front. Sidewalks were buckled in places.

All in all, the place was a dump. Of course, this wasn't her part of town. This was the part of town she rarely entered and never talked about. The closer they got to the courthouse, the more seediness she saw.

"Why don't people take care of this sort of thing?" She didn't expect an answer and was surprised when the officer told her a lot of people were out of work. "I don't believe that. Some of these people look as if they've just rolled out of bed. It's nearly two in the afternoon. What are they? Drunks? Dopers? It's disgusting."

"Some of these people worked at the basket plant for a lot of years. Now that it's closed down, it's difficult for them to find jobs. You'd know that if you were to get your head out of your butt and be a part of the town you live in. I'm betting when you want new clothing, it never occurs to you to buy locally." Fran asked her why on earth she'd think that would be a good idea. "Because believe it or not, there are a lot of people here that are as talented if not more so than anyone in a larger city. You just think, like most rich, that if it's expensive, it has to be the best."

"Well, of course, that's right. You pay for what you

get. If something is cheap, it's cheaply made. I don't even know why others don't know that. Surely you don't pay second rate prices on the things you buy." The officer told her she was on a budget. "Yes, well, my husband made more than enough money for me to never have to worry about things like that. My daughter and I had a lot of fun being the family of a rich man."

"Don't you have two daughters?" Fran glared at the woman. "Sure, you do. I've met her. Amy is a wonderful person. Did you know she's getting married?"

"She is married — this morning. I was there picking up my assignments for today, and I saw them. Amy was a beautiful bride. All those Wilkerson men standing up for their cousin was a sight to behold. What I wouldn't give to have a single date with one of those hunky men." The driver, another female officer, looked at Fran in the rearview mirror. "Not that I think you'll give a good fig, but Amy has a wonderful husband now and someone that will care for her for the rest of her life."

"I have that too." Both women snorted at her. "You're referring, no doubt, to the rumors going around that Shelton is divorcing me. That's not true. He loves me. Well, I don't know if he actually ever loved me, but we're used to things the way they've been. You'll see. Once I'm out of jail, he'll be there to pamper me to no end. He's just been listening to things that Amy told him. That girl never liked me."

"Even though you're her mother? Amy doesn't strike

me as a person who would just not like someone for no reason. What did you do to her to make her dislike you?"

"Nothing. What a thing to say to me. I think it's about time you minded your own p's and q's up there and leave me to my thoughts. To think that someone actually pays the two of you for sitting around on your asses all day and spreading gossip. Just wait until I tell Shelton. He'll have your jobs taken from you so quickly, you're not going to be able to say anything."

"Yes, well, I'm doubting very few things you have in your head are going to come to pass, Fran. You're going to be serving a little bit more jail time for your little prank last night." Fran told the woman to not call her by her given name. She wasn't her peer. "Peer or not, you'll do as I tell you or I'll have to get all business-like on your ass. I'm the one in charge today, and the sooner you remember I carry a gun and a Taser, the sooner you're going to be able to go back to your cell unharmed today."

Fran didn't bother arguing with them. She knew her rights, and she also knew she had Shelton right where she wanted him. He'd be able to carry on without her, she knew that, but she made him look good when they were out on company functions. Told him the names of people that were around him. Fran was his ally when it came to social functions too. He'd be the laughingstock of the entire county if she didn't keep him in line.

When they stopped in the parking lot behind the courthouse, Fran looked around for her daughter. She wanted to see Phoenix, to find out if she was being treated well.

Instead of seeing the daughter she loved, sometimes more than money, she saw Amy. There were several large men around her today. While she had no idea why anyone would want to be seen in public with the wretch, there they were, falling all over themselves like puppies at a tit. Men were so stupid.

Then she noticed Amy was in a wheelchair. Her leg was wrapped up in some sort of plaster thing, and she was being lifted, chair and all, up to the landing where the back doors were that she was being led to.

Jerking on the chain to get the other women to stop, they both turned to her and asked her if she wanted to be dragged in. Shaking her head, they jerked on the chains harder, making her fall down in the gravel.

"Now look what you've done." She sat up, not an easy thing with chains on her wrists and ankles. "Help me up, you idiots. You'll have to take me back to the jail. I'm not going to be seen in this mess you've made of me. Look here. You've broken the skin on both my knees, and it's ruined my stockings. Take me back. Better yet, take me by my home, and I'll get what I need there. Of all the stupidity. What were you thinking?"

Not only did they help her up, one of them nearly tossed her on top of the car nearby, she'd been jerked up so hard. As it was, she was off balance and nearly fell again when she was told she was scheduled to go in now. Not after she had herself a pamper party.

"Pamper party? Is that what you call getting cleaned up for an outing? Good Christ, woman, don't you ever think about the appearances you make when you're out? That's all I can think about." The driver told her it mattered little where she was going. "It matters to me. I demand you take me by my home so I can get cleaned up and fix my makeup. I cannot believe you don't have some makeup for people like me to use when they have a visitor."

"What sort of person do you think you are? A jailbird? A convict? A divorced woman? You're all those things before you're anything else in my book." Fran told her she didn't care for her book. "Well, isn't that just too bad for you. You're not going to your home. I'm not even sure if you'll have one after today. Get your butt in gear, or I'll drag your fat ass right into this courtroom and not care a bit if you're dirty or have a boo-boo that you need to have looked at. Now. It's up to you. Walk or dragged? I don't have all day."

Not only was she dragged into the building, but each time Fran fell on one of the larger rocks in the lot, she would be pulled across the lot until the other officer helped her up. Again and again, she demanded to be taken home, and each time they both ignored her in favor of humiliating her in front of anyone around. Not that she cared if the poor saw what she looked like, but there were people there, mostly her friends, who were going to see her in a not so nice look. Damn this shit, Fran thought. She was going to do some serious looking into some petty lives when she was free from this place. And she would be too. There was no way that Shelton would leave her hanging like some sort of degenerate.

Fran was seated in a little room that had several chairs in it, all of them with large round eye bolts screwed into the floor like the ones in the van. She was shoved into one of the chairs then bolted to the floor, like a wild animal.

"You don't have to do this to me. I think you've done enough to show you think you're better than I am. Little things like this only show how ignorant you are about the class differences we have." The woman asked her where she thought she was in the class differences. "Well above you, that's for sure."

"Are you now? Well, perhaps you should have another look, Fran. I'm not the one wearing chains and being watched over by armed guards." She laughed as she stood up. "You might well have more money than I do, but you certainly don't have any manners. I think that's just on you and your daughter Phoenix. Amy must have been raised by someone else. It surely couldn't have been you. You're a terrible person."

Not dignifying anything she said with a comeback, Fran closed her mouth. When they laughed at her, she knew they'd get what was coming to them as soon as she got into the courtroom. A tell-all was going to be forthcoming, and they'd both be fired by the end of the day. Either she'd do it, or she'd have Shelton do it. Either way, it was a done deal.

It was another forty-five minutes before she was moved into the courtroom. Once there, she thought for sure she'd be released to have a little bit of dignity. But no, she was not only taken there in the heavy chains, but she was locked to the table, so she wasn't even able to scratch her nose if she wanted. Fran could not understand why they were treating her this way. She'd not done a damned thing wrong except hurting, not killing, Amy's husband.

The first person she saw when she was finished being chained was Phoenix. She, too, was being treated poorly. The second person was Doug, the man who'd skipped out on marrying her daughter. Amy was also in the room, again with all those men. Fran wondered which one she'd married, if any of them.

Today was going to be enlightening to a great many people, especially those who'd tried to take advantage of her while Shelton got his shit together. After today she was going to make sure he understood that if she wasn't happy, he was going to be extremely unhappy. Or dead. Right now, to her, it was looking like he was going to be pushing up roses. Daises were so cheap in her book. Hell, they even grew along the side of the road. No, he'd be pushing up roses even if she had to plant them herself.

Chapter 7

North wasn't sure where he'd lost control, but it was sort of funny too. The bailiff had helped him add chairs to his side of the table. Not only was his dad there, but all four of his uncles, Shelton, and Amy. Only because there wasn't any place for her to sit on the other side of the room while she was in her wheelchair.

When the judge was seated, she cocked a brow at him. "Is an invasion going to happen here today, Mr. Wilkerson? Or have you decided to have all your family here to celebrate your birthday or something?"

"No, ma'am. They're here for support, they told me." She looked at the men and waved back at his dad when he waved at her. "I believe we're working up to becoming Wilkersons and Son soon."

"Are they the silent part of the Wilkersons? From what I've heard, the lot of them have been having a wonderful time since they've been released from their marital bonds. I'm happy for them, but see no reason for them to have to sit in a courtroom all day." He nodded, and all of them explained how they were here for each other, talking over one another and getting louder each time they were making a point. "I guess I was wrong. They're not all that silent, are they?"

"No, Your Honor. More the overly opinionated part of the firm. I'm enjoying their input, if nothing else. It's nice having them around. Don't you think?" She said it was even better to see them smiling again. "Yes, I must agree with you there. But they are here for support. If you'd rather they took another place to support from afar, I'm sure they'll move."

"No, I sort of like seeing a supportive family. In my line of work, I see more splitting of a family rather than something like this." She looked at his mother-in-law, Fran, and then at Phoenix. "I'm thinking this is just the kind of case I was thinking about. Well, what are we taking on first here? Divorce, hit and run, or damage and attempted murder?"

"I'm sorry. I thought this was just for the divorce." She picked up the folders that had been handed to her and looked them over. "I wasn't prepared to handle the other cases today. I'm not saying I won't, I just hadn't been made aware of the changes."

"Give me a moment, North." He knew this woman well. Her Honorable Lorinda Wessex had taught at the college where he'd gone for a long time until her promotion to the bench. He knew her to be fair and smart. She was also a no-nonsense type of judge. "From what I'm seeing here, it looks like it won't take you much in prep work. If it looks like it's not going to work, I'll reschedule the other hearing. You tell me when we get to them if you feel like you can handle it. I'm sure some of the staff you have there can make you some notes on it."

All five of them nodded and pulled out their briefcases. So he'd not laugh with Amy when she snickered, he turned his back to them and looked at the judge. She, too, was having a hard time maintaining control over her humor.

"Your Honor, we're here today to discuss violations of the prenup of Ms. Francine Small Hamilton, as well as to execute a divorce from Mr. Shelton Hamilton." Fran said she wasn't there to divorce anyone. Ignoring her, he moved on with his claims. "I have evidence to support that Francine has violated seventeen of the twenty-one points of the prenup that could be grounds for divorce. I'm aware this is a no-fault state. But for purposes of Mr. Hamilton retaining his wealth, it needs to be brought up just how much has been done to ruin this union."

He handed a copy of the list to not just Fran, but the judge as well. Starting with the most recent violation, North was thrilled he'd be able to bring out the pictures to show just what sort of depraved woman Fran was.

"On August tenth of this year, Ms. Hamilton, as well as Mrs. Hamilton, engaged in a—for lack of a better word, Your Honor, an orgy." He handed Lorinda the photos first, then to Fran and Phoenix. "This caused the young

Mr. Doug Schmidt to not only back out of the wedding that was to be executed in two days but also Mr. Hamilton to be left to pay for the wedding that had gone well over budget that was no longer going to happen."

"Excuse me. I didn't really want to marry him in the first place. He was just a starting point for me to work my way up to someone old and rich. Like a sugar daddy." Phoenix smiled at Lorinda like this was something special. "And none of this would have happened had it not been for that stupid cow over there. If she'd done what I wanted and hadn't bitched about the pictures *I* wanted to be taken, then Daddy wouldn't be stuck with a wedding that didn't happen. People need to remember that I'm the bride."

"What person are you calling the cow, Ms. Hamilton?" Abby stood up, and he winked at her as the judge continued. "Mrs. Wilkerson, did you take these photos as well? There are some good shots in them."

Amy and he snickered.

"No, Your Honor. Those were taken at the home of Mr. Hamilton. Shelton called me the night before I was to take the wedding pictures and warned me that things might not go as was contracted. We did have a contract, and both the Hamilton women didn't want me to stick to what they'd ordered. I called Shelton when things began to look savage, and that was when I was informed my services were no longer needed." Lorinda asked if she'd been paid. "Yes, Your Honor. With a bonus for having to put up with the two of them. If you don't mind my saying this, they're not the nicest people you could ever want to be around."

"Well, I mind you saying that. You should have just done what I wanted, and that would have been the end of things. As it is now, I'm stuck in jail for trying to keep my honor intact." North heard Amy say something like *"good luck with that,"* but he didn't acknowledge it. He was still trying to not burst out laughing at the two women who were going back to jail. Hopefully. "When is this charade going to be over with? I want to go home and take a bath. Wear my own clothing. As it is now, I'm going to have to have the hospital look at my wounds. Those officers treated me like I was nothing more than...well, a criminal."

"You are a criminal. Now, hush up and let me see what else is going on here." North waited for Fran to say something more, but she only sat there glaring at Lorinda. "Mr. Wilkerson, please go on with what you have there."

North was going over the things purchased with Shelton's credit cards that had been for other men when Lorinda asked him to stop. She asked him how many more items he had on his list.

"Ten more. All basically things that were specially mentioned as grounds for divorce, as well as reasons for no alimony to be paid out. I also have a list of things his daughter, Phoenix, had done to make sure she doesn't get anything from the estate."

"What? Wait a minute. I didn't sign anything that says I'm going to have to follow rules. You have to support me, Daddy. I don't have anything to fall back on. What will

I do while living in the house with you? You don't want me to be bored, do you?" North said she was forty years old. "You keep your fucking mouth shut. I'll deal with you later. Of all the nerve of some people. What does it matter to you where I live anyway? My daddy will take me in simply because I'm his daughter."

"So is Amy."

North was sure that had Phoenix been able to stand up, she would have flown across the room and torn him apart. As it was, all she did was use every combination of curse words he'd ever heard. His favorite by far, before she was told to shut up, was *fucking waddle duck*. He was going to have to remember that when he needed a good laugh.

The judge took over from there. "I've seen enough. Mr. Hamilton, would you please stand?" Shelton did, and so did everyone at his table. "I can see right here that you're going to have all the support you'll ever need in this family. I also want to congratulate you on getting a wonderful son-in-law in North Wilkerson. I am granting you your divorce. There will be no waiting period, nor will there be any payments made out to either your ex-wife or your daughter. Good luck, sir. I believe you're going to need it after today."

The room erupted in cheers. The only people not happy were Fran and Phoenix. When Lorinda asked him if he was ready for the next bit of Hamilton drama, his dad stood up.

"I'm going to take that case, Your Honor. I've been talking a great deal with Shelton here, and I think I can make a good case on behalf of him." Lorinda said she didn't doubt that one bit. "Thank you, Your Honor. I might need some reminders about a few minor things as we go."

Within minutes the courtroom resembled a bar fight on a Friday night. Not nearly as destructive, but just as loud with name-calling and threats. Through it all, his dad and uncles sat there, cool as they could be, just watching the two women try and get to each other to beat the other down. North went to sit with his wife and held her hand.

"Is this something that happens a great deal to you?" North told Amy he'd never been more entertained than he was at this very moment. "Watch it, buddy, or they'll have you locked up right beside them."

"I'm not worried. I know you'll come save me." North watched as Lorinda tried to regain control of the room. When her gavel broke and went flying across the room, Amy grabbed it out of the air one-handed, like a professional first baseman. "Good job. If the photography business ever takes a dive, you could probably get a position on the Cleveland Indians team."

"Shut up!" The room was as silent as a funeral home when Lorinda stood up, yelling. "Bailiff, I want you to take these two women back to their respective jail cells. Perhaps then we can get some work done around here."

"I'm not going back to jail. I have a great many things to do. Since you arbitrarily granted my husband a divorce, which you can bet I'm going to dispute, I need to make arrangements to get my things. Who knows how long it will be before I can get someone to help me sue this idiot for doing me so wrong?"

"I've given it all away." Fran looked at Shelton and asked him what he'd said. "I did. I decided it was a terrible reminder of how you screwed me over with purchasing other men's suits, so I had a service come and pack it all up and take it all to a second-hand shop. All of Phoenix's things as well. I have to tell you both, it was the most liberating thing I've ever done. That is if you don't count my getting you two harpies out of my life."

North stood up and made his way back to his table. He had no idea why, but he had an awful feeling the shit was about to be rained down on Shelton like he'd never felt before. Even Amy, wheelchair and all, was making a move.

As soon as he stood between Shelton and Fran, the seat she was sitting in toppled over and dumped her and Phoenix to the floor. North saw Amy pull her dad back out of reach just as the bailiff moved to untangle the two women. Dad was gathering the uncles up and pushing the table away from the mess on the floor.

Just as the judge stood up to leave the courtroom, a gun fired in North's direction. Not at all sure who had shot the gun, he saw it between the police officer's legs. Grabbing it before it went off again, he just missed being shot in the hand when it fired the second time. Wrestling it away from the hand, he heard bones break, and it was apparent to him that it was a woman's hand. Other than that, he knew very little.

It took another ten minutes to get Fran out of the courtroom. She was still screaming about her rights and her things when the officer went to get Phoenix up from the floor. North had broken her wrist, perhaps even a couple of fingers by the look of it. When a medic was called, no one moved from their position when more police arrived.

"Are you all right?" North said he thought so, but did circle around so that Amy could make sure. "Where the hell did she get that fucking gun? I thought they checked people out when they got in here. They sure gave me the once over."

Just as North was explaining that she'd gotten it from one of the officers, a scream went up. Turning to protect Amy at all costs, the bailiff told everyone to stay back. Lorinda had been shot.

"I'm a doctor." Wats came from the visitor's seats. "Mars has gone to get my bag. Everyone, please give me some room to work."

North helped by talking to Lorinda and telling her how good Wats was, and that he'd have her up and around in no time. She was lying on her belly, but to him, it looked as if she were bleeding from the front. As he wasn't a doctor, North kept his thoughts to himself. He had a feeling, however, that Lorinda wasn't going to make it. There was a great deal of blood surrounding her, and

Wats was covered in it. Wats never stopped working to save the woman until the ambulance arrived.

Wats was barking orders to the EMTs as they hooked her up with an IV and a heart monitor. It was, surprisingly, a slow but steady beat sounding from the machine. When they were ready to get her out of the room. Lorinda grabbed North before they put her in the ambulance.

"Call Charlie." He said he would. "My cell. On my desk. Tell her, I love her." North told her she could tell her when she was out of surgery. "Don't shit me. I know better. Call my Charlie."

North stood there with a heavy heart. He, too, knew better. Lorinda wasn't going to make it. And having to call her daughter and tell her what had happened was going to break a lot of people's hearts.

~*~

Amy was ready to call it a night when North finally called her from the hospital. She'd had him go to the hospital with his friend instead of worrying about her. Hank had taken her to get some dinner and had brought her home. The others had joined them, and she spent an enjoyable night with her new uncles and her dad.

"She's holding her own right now. Wats said the next twenty-four hours will tell. I hadn't realized she'd been shot in the back until we got to the hospital." Amy asked him if he'd called her daughter. "Yes. She is renting a car to use while she's here as soon as her plane lands. When I told her what had happened, she said her mom would make it. She was tough as nails."

"I spoke to your dad about what went down tonight. Phoenix is being charged with the attempted murder of a federal judge. I didn't know she was federal, did you?" North told her he'd read about her title a few months ago. "I don't think we're going to have to worry about her for a while. Your dad told me she'll get the big-time sentence for this. Attempted murder is bad enough, but nearly killing a sitting judge is triple that."

"I did manage to break her wrist, and three of her fingers, one of the emergency doctors told me." Amy told him she wished it had been her that had done it. "I'm glad she didn't get near you. She would have hurt you worse with you unable to get up and around. Listen, I'm going to head home here in about ten minutes. I want to check on Charlie once more." She told him to be careful driving and that she'd see him soon. "Not much of a wedding night, is it, love?"

"We're together, and that is really all I wanted. It's not been the best of beginnings, but it'll be better after this. I'm sure of it." North told her again how much he loved her. "I love you forever. And a day." When he told her again that he was leaving soon, they hung up.

Amy thought about what her mother had told her when she'd called her this evening. It had taken her a few rings to know if she wanted to answer a call from the jail but figured there was no way she could physically hurt her over the phone.

"You're to tell your father I'm not going to put up with this. You tell him it's going to cost him for giving away all my things." Amy told her mother she doubted he'd care. "He will care when he realizes just how much I've been doing for him over the years. Who do you think made sure he was presentable when he went out? It certainly wasn't him. He couldn't match a shirt to a tie to save his life. You'll see. Mark my words, he'll be begging me to return home."

"If I were you, I'd not hold my breath on that happening. Or you could. That would suit us both if you were to keep holding your breath." Mother called her ungrateful. "Perhaps in your mind. But you'll be surprised to learn that I don't care what you think about me at all. Not that you've ever cared for me. But as for your feelings for me, I've not cared for a very long time."

"You see, right there. That's the very reason I've always hated you, Amy. You go on about how much you don't care, yet I've seen how you suck up to your father when you don't think anyone is looking." Even though she'd known her mother didn't like her, it hurt Amy to her very core to hear her say the words. "For once in your life, do what I tell you, or so help me, Amy, you'll regret it."

"No." Her mother told her it wasn't any time for her to be smart assed. "I'm not. Also, I'm not going to be taking your demands to Dad or anyone else. In fact, I'm going to make you aware of something right now, Mother. I'm finished with you and Phoenix. As far as I'm concerned, you're both dead. Also, today Phoenix shot a judge. She's going to go to federal prison for that, for a minimum of fifty years. I hope they give her the maximum. You? Well, it matters little to me, but you're going to go away for a long time as well. You have a nice life, the two of you."

Hanging up on her mother had been empowering. Not only did she feel good about that, but she was going to have her number changed. She'd have her dad do the same thing. Tomorrow was going to be a day of getting things going her way.

Closing her eyes, she thought about relaxing each part of her body, her toes first, then her ankles and up her legs. The more she moved up her body, the more she realized this was working much better than it had in the past. When she felt all the tension around her neck and shoulders let go, Amy let sleep take her under. She barely remembered North coming in and kissing her. Sleep was much too strong to pass up when her body felt this good.

Waking up, a warm body touching hers, Amy rolled onto her back and moaned when strong hands massaged her waist. It was a wonderful feeling when North's hand, that was all it could be, moved up from around her waist to her breasts.

"Who would have believed a woman's breast would feel so tense? Thank you for helping me out with that." He told her he could work on them closely for her. "Oh, yes. You do that for me."

His sexy laughter made her body warm. When his tongue touched her tight nipple, she moaned again, this time feeling his warm sigh when it blew over her wet nipple.

"You're very responsive. I love that about you." Amy told North if he made her scream, she'd make it worth his time. "Oh, I think I can do that for you. How many times would you like to release for me, Amy? I have all day." Instead of answering him, she moaned again. Amy was too relaxed, too everything, to come up with an answer that would have made sense to anyone. "I love you. I am in love with you so very much."

Amy wasn't prepared for him touching her clit with his mouth. It sent a wave of something powerful though her entire body, from one heartbeat to the next. Screaming wasn't even possible. Her breath, her heart, not one thing on her worked when he commanded her to come a second, more powerful time.

The world spun off its axis. Time seemed to have stilled, so there was no sound, not even a slight breeze blowing over the bed. When North told her to come for the third time, she bowed up off the bed, this time screaming the pleasure, the very soul of herself out her mouth into the room, shattering all ability to think past the pleasure North was giving her. Amy begged him to stop.

"Oh, no. I don't think so. We're just getting started, and this was your idea." When he suckled at her clit again, she had no strength to beg him to stop. Even if there had been even a little, she wouldn't have been able to use it. "Come for me, Amy mine. Come now."

There was no reprieve, nothing to stop him from giving her everything she had asked him for, needed, or even had inside of her. They'd been teasing each other for days, tantalizing, flirting, and touching since they'd met. Their first kiss had been leading up to this. The first time they'd touched had been a precursor to their life together.

His body crawling up her body, touching her with his hands and mouth, Amy sobbed at how overwhelmed she was with the emotions. Too many nerve endings were firing at once. Each time his breath touched her skin, it was like a flame was set to her. Not just a fire, but love too.

"I want you." Nodding, she received him with her mouth and her body. His cock filled not just her body, but some unknown need that she knew only he'd ever fill. "Take me, Amy. Let us be one, now and forever."

Not holding anything back, Amy held him to her, took everything his body was offering up to her, and gave all she was back in return. Screaming out her love for him, he did the same. Amy felt her world dip and twist. As soon as he came again, Amy let go of herself and simply slipped away on a wave of complete bliss.

There was movement beside her. The sound of soft male laughter made her smile. Then Amy found herself wrapped tightly in his big arms, snuggled into his warm chest. Just before she fell asleep again, the kiss to her shoulder had her turning to him for more.

"Christ, I love you."

Amy told North how much she loved him before she

fell back to sleep in the arms of the only man she'd ever love.

Chapter 8

North felt like he was walking on sunshine. That song, from long ago, came to his mind with every thought he had of his wife. Even to think that he was a married man would give him tingles all the way down his spine.

"You're in a good mood." North told his dad he was in love. "Any fool can see that, son. But today you seem to be brighter. More of…I was going to say like your old self, but I just realized I don't know what that would be. More than likely, I'd say you were like you would have been when you were staying with my sister."

"This is better. But I did like staying with Aunt Holly. She could and did make me feel like a person. I didn't feel that at home. Mother, she would take good news, good feelings, and tear them to shreds. She would also beat me. As I got older, she would have someone do it, but she made it perfectly clear she was the one that would order it. Mom watched and cheered them on." North realized he was bringing them both down. "Aunt Holly could cook like a chef. I'm not kidding, Dad, she made these homemade noodles that were so buttery and tender, I swear to you, it put me off of store-bought ones forever. And her Alfredo sauce? Christ, it was heaven in a saucepan."

"Yeah? Your grandma was a good cook. I bet Holly learned it from her. You should have tasted Grandma's chocolate chip cookies, son. You'd swear she put something magical in them that would have you craving more." Dad smiled at him, his memories evident on his face. "Once, when we were all at my grandma's—I think I was about thirteen then—we had this wonderful dish. Oh my, son, if I could have one meal that I had when I was a kid, that would be it. She would take a steak and pound it into these big steak-like meats, bread it, and then fry it in bacon grease. She'd serve it up with mashed potatoes with the skins still on some of them. And this thing—I swear to you, it was made from the gods—that she simply called white gravy. It was a meal fit for a king."

"I can make that. With fresh green beans that have simmered all day with ham bits in them. And a cake-like cornbread on the side." Dad stared at him with his mouth open. "Aunt Holly told each of us that someday it might become necessary for us to impress someone. Be it a woman or anyone, we should at least know how to care for ourselves. I can cook several meals like that one. Bake a loaf or two of bread, and make any kind of sweet cookie you'd want to sink your teeth into. She also made sure we could do our own laundry and make a bed."

"We're having it as soon as it can be arranged." North laughed. "No. You have no idea how serious I am right now. I'll go into town and pick up everything you need. You invite the others over, all right? From what I heard yesterday, your house is all finished up. You go ahead and take that girl of yours to the store and order what furniture you need to have company. I'll pay for the extra delivery to have it in there by today."

"Dad, slow down." His dad was giddy, a word he'd never thought to associate with him. "I'll go and pick up Amy, and we'll go shopping. Are you still going to stay with us for a little while, or are you going to keep living in the condo? These are things that need to be taken care of one at a time."

"Yes. I love living in the condo. To be honest with you, son, I'm enjoying the alone time. I love that it's just the right size for me too. An added bonus is that all my brothers are close enough to walk over and see. Did I tell you I'm going with Josiah to see Christa tomorrow?" North asked him if he thought that was a good idea. "No. Neither one of us thinks it is, but he said he needs some closure. I think, with the way things were going at the end there between your mother and me, I got to have something they didn't. I got to see firsthand what she was really like. I know I should have seen it all along, but I had a clear view of what I should have been taking care of from the very first time you came to me."

North didn't even bother telling his father he was sorry,

because frankly, he wasn't. His mother had made her bed and had been murdered for her ways. Not on purpose. Mom had been killed by one of the other wives. However it happened, his mother was no longer a threat to any of them, especially to Mars. But the other wives, wives of his uncles, were making threats of their own.

"Tina called my cell phone the other day. She left a message telling me I'd better be getting my ducks in a row, that she was going to be in charge, and all my slacking off, she called it, was coming to an end. She also mentioned she was moving into the big house as soon as you gathered your stuff up. Being the second oldest, Uncle Wesley should be moved into it. For some reason, she has this idea that since you're no longer married, you have to move out. I've told her Mars is now living in it, but she doesn't want to hear that, so it's not registering to her, I guess." Dad asked him how she thought she was going to be moving anywhere but to a larger prison. "I don't know, to be honest with you. I think each of them are under the assumption they're getting out of jail soon. I've heard that Penelope called and left a message for Shawn to have him bring her some of her clothing and jewelry. When she got home, she told him, she was going to look good."

"Perhaps we should have a talk with all of them. I know there have been other calls to you boys." North told him there were several calls a week to one or more of them. "Yes, they only get phone time once a week. I suppose they could be calling their sons and leaving the same sort of message for them. I'm going to talk to my attorney about this. We need to, I guess, for lack of a better term, set them straight. I know we've all done this individually, but it's not sticking. There has to be an end to this nonsense right now."

When he pulled up in front of the house, North asked his dad if he wanted to go with him and Amy to shop. He thought for sure he was going to turn him down, but after a few minutes, he nodded and said he wanted to go. He wanted to make his own statement.

Not having any idea what he meant, Dad went to his condo to pick up a few things, and North went into his home. Amy was just being fitted for crutches with Wats. She was doing a good job of it, and Wats was clearly happy with her healing. North told them both what they were going to do.

"Take the wheelchair with you, Amy. I don't want you to get exhausted too soon and hurt yourself again." She said she was thinking that as well. "Good. You'll heal better, as you are now because you're not rushing things. I wish I had more patients doing that."

North told his cousin what he and his dad had talked about. "You need to let Abby and me go down there and have a meeting with them. I'm sure we can knock some sense into their heads." North laughed and asked Amy if she'd be actually knocking them around. "If they need to be. I think you guys are still slightly afraid of them. I know I would be if that were me. I'm still afraid of my mom, even though I know there isn't really a good reason for me to be anymore. Not with them both in jail."

"You can talk to my dad while we go shopping. I think he's just fed up with all of them. I know my mom is gone, but as the oldest, I think he still feels like he should be in charge of the family. Not that I can find fault with that. But I don't want him to be too stressed out either. He can't die on me, guys. I'm having too much fun just getting to know him." Wats said he and his dad were having dinner twice a week now, and that was something he'd been enjoying too. "I think we're all having fun. I know Dad is enjoying his time with Mars. I think Mars has been pulling out some of the pictures Aunt Holly was forever taking and showing them to him. He shares a story too. I've been doing that with my dad as well."

"I'll have to get with him and get some of the pictures too. Are they still in those big albums?"

North explained to Amy that Aunt Holly would print every picture she took, no matter if they were from a camera or her phone, and put them into an album. Watts laughed as he continued the story.

"Each year, there would be a new album. She even had us write something about the pictures we were in. At first, I thought of it as dumb. But later on, when we'd be looking over the older pictures, I could see my comments and wonder why I was such a teenager. Aunt Holly never told us what to say. I think I'll do something like that for my own kids. Wouldn't it be wonderful to have a yearly album still?" Amy said they had two photographers in the family, they'd better bet there would be pictures. "We should have some taken of all of us. I mean, with our dads. What do you think? Each year we get together at the mansion, take the picture in the same spot, and make that the first picture in the books."

"I love that idea." He did too. North said he'd have to talk with Mars. Amy said she'd do it. She needed to speak to him about a couple of things anyway, regarding an upcoming wedding. "You getting married again? I think it's a little soon for us to be thinking of renewing our vows, don't you?"

"It is. But have you seen the garden in the back of the house?" North said he'd grown up there. "Yes, well, Abby hired some firm to come in and make it fresh. And holy smokes, it's really beautiful now. I wanted to find out if I could take a few engagement photos there sometimes. Not all of them. Also, a few wedding shots. The way they have it situated back there now, you can barely see the house for all the flowers."

"I'll have to check it out."

Dad came over about the time he got the wheelchair loaded up in the truck. North was glad now that he'd gotten a larger bed on his truck. It was making things like this possible. Amy hugged his dad, and they both helped her into the back seat where she could stretch out.

"I think I might need to think about getting us a car too. Perhaps for Amy to get around in."

"I just heard from Mars while I was at the house. He wanted to know if I wanted any of the cars in the garage. To be honest with you, I had completely forgotten there were old cars stored in that thing. After we get back, you should go and look them over. I believe Mars has decided to see if Amy or Abby would like to use them for wedding pictures."

He told his dad what they'd been talking about. "I wonder if they'll go into business together. I mean, they're in different fields of the same thing, but it might do them some good to start their own studio around here. Sure would keep them home more." Dad laughed with him. "I'll talk to them all when we have the dinner you want to have."

The three of them enjoyed the drive to the furniture store. Even more so when it seemed his dad had way different tastes than they did. North did ask him if he'd been out and about lately, and he told him he'd not been to a furniture store in over thirty years.

"Sorry, buster, but it shows." Dad laughed with Amy. "You need to get out more. I know you're doing better, but you still are behind in the times. Speaking of which, you need to upgrade your wardrobe. It's all right to wear sandals, but when you wear dress socks with them, you start to age yourself. And it's completely acceptable to not have three million pockets in your shorts."

"I have a lot of stuff to carry around." She asked him what. "Tissues, my wallet. I also need my sunglasses. Then there is—" Amy put up her hand. "What if I just got me one of those man purses? How would that work?"

"You do that, and I'll have you committed. Christ man. Did you ever pick out something you wanted to wear? Something comfy? Do you even own a pair of gym shorts?" Dad asked Amy what those were. North had a feeling his father really didn't have a clue what she was referring to. "You own any jeans? Anything that you could consider sloppy?"

"No. I mean, I have been wearing a tie since I was old enough to tie one." She asked him if he wore a tie at home. "Sure. I mean, what if someone showed up and I had to talk to them?"

"Then you say, 'I'm fucking taking some time off, and if you don't care for my mode of dress, then fuck off.'" Dad said he could never say that. "I think you just need to forget what other people think about what you're wearing and start dressing in comfort. You don't have a job that you have to dress up for. There aren't that many meetings you have to attend where you need to have a suit on to make sure you're ready to go. When we've picked out enough furniture for the house, we're taking you shopping for something fun. You do remember what fun is, don't you?"

"I'll have to try and remember, but yes, I've been known to have some fun in my day." She asked him if he dressed in a suit when he did. "You know, it is quite possible to have fun while wearing a suit, young lady."

"No, it's not. It's completely not possible to wear any

kind of matching clothing and have fun. At least real fun. Fun to most people isn't sitting around the house and reading about who you can throw out of the orphanages today." Dad told her she was a little harsh. "No. I'm not. You, my dear father-in-law, have been stifled way too long. You need to let out the inner bad boy in you. I bet you could be the life of the party if you were to let your hair hang down."

"North, I think your wife is trying to change me." North told his dad he did need to be updated. "You two are making me sound like an old computer. Update indeed."

When he walked away, North looked at Amy when she said his name. "We have enough for now. Go and take your dad shopping. Please? He really does need something fun if he's going to talk to the others' wives. He needs to show them he's got his shit together, and they can suck a big dick if they have shit to say about it." North cocked his brow at her. "I've been hanging out with Abby. But I do have a reason for being this way about your dad. Did you hear that the women are trying to find a hitman to take out Mars again? Abby said the police called the house yesterday and told Mars about it. He's pretty upset, but didn't want you guys to know."

"Why not?" Amy told him she wasn't sure, but it had to be out there. "I agree with you. Mars isn't alone in this anymore. Not that he ever was, but we're all here for him, including his uncles. You're right about them. They can suck a big dick if they want things to go their way."

"That's my man." She asked him if he thought she'd upset his dad. North told her he didn't think so. "I love him too. I hope he knows I just want him to feel like he's cutting away from the old him."

"I'll talk to him. I promise he'll find something new to wear. It's doubtful my mom would have allowed him to have worn anything but suits all the time." Amy told him how much she loved him. "And I love you. You and Abby have been great for this family. I can only imagine what the next woman will bring to the table."

They were both still laughing when they caught up with his dad. Dad had been a little upset, but he told Amy he was sorry. Also that she was right. After that, Dad kept an open mind and an open mouth. He was very vocal to them about what he wanted in new duds, he called them, for himself.

~*~

Amy found herself at the prison the next afternoon. Tonight she was going to sit back and watch six grown men make dinner. She didn't have any doubt they could do it, but she was really concerned for the mess they might make while doing it. Her dad was also going to enjoy the fun. She and Abby were in charge of desserts. But a call from the prison regarding her mother had her hitching a ride from Abby to see what her mother could possibly want.

"I'm going to have a little talk with Tina and Penny. By the way, you have to call them that if you want to piss them off. What do you call your mom to make her mad?" Amy said, Mom. "Are you kidding? She doesn't want you to call her Mom? That's really tough on you, I bet."

"Not so much anymore. When I was younger, it was, but now, I just don't care. I think that's what really bothered them too, my mom and sister. It's that I literally do not give a crap what they think about me." But she knew it had hurt her. Abby had been a good person to cry to when she got off the phone with her mom. "What are you going to say to them? Any notes?"

"I'm going to tell them to stop fucking calling the house and upsetting my husband for starters. How they got the new number is beyond me. I'm going to have to do some house cleaning of staff if they get this one." Amy told her she'd have fired them all anyway. "I think it's going to come to that. Some of them are very loyal to the other women. But a lot of them are coming around. I've told Mars that we could maybe change their minds, but I'm not having the best of luck."

They were sitting at one of the tables, waiting on her mom to show up, when Abby got a phone call. As she walked away, Amy's mom was seated across from her and chained to the floor. Amy didn't say a word to her until the officer walked away.

"Why the hell am I still here? Does anyone out there care that I don't belong in here?" Amy told her she doubted that anyone had missed her. "You're a crude bitch. I know better. Why, I've gotten at least three calls a day since I've been in here from my friends. That's all I'm allowed, or there would be more, and you know it."

"What I know is that you've not gotten a single call in here since you've arrived and that not one of your so-called friends is the least bit surprised to find out that you're on that side of the bars. What is it you want that has me dragged down here when I have better things to do? Like I have a dentist appointment later today that I'm looking forward to more than I am talking to you right now." Mom told her to shut up. "Gladly. Does that mean you won't be calling me anymore? Or having the police call me? I really am sick of hearing about how you were wrongly accused of what has you in here." She said she needed to get home. "To what? There is nothing left there for you. As you've been told, the house is being stripped down to the walls, and Dad is making it more like he wants it. You have nothing in the house that didn't come from Dad, so you're not going to even get anything like some dirty underwear you might have left behind. That wasn't a joke, by the way. They did find some of your nasty thongs in your bathroom when it was cleaned out."

"You tell him I want everything put back where it was. He's not to touch my things." Amy asked her if she thought he'd turn into something by touching her things. "What do you mean, turn into something?"

"I don't know, Mother. Do you expect that unlike everyone else in this world, your nasty shit should be put on display so all those who come after you can be impressed? No one would be just so you know. I'm certainly not. Besides, Dad isn't touching anything. He's having a group of people in hazmat suits cleaning your rooms." Amy laughed at the expression on her mother's face. "Also, you should be aware that Phoenix's things have been removed. Going into her rooms now is like she's never been there. There were some laughs because of the posters she still had on the walls. I think some of the bands she had hanging there have been broken up longer than I've been alive."

"I swear to you, Amy, you're going to regret doing all this. I'm going to make you pay for every little thing that is missing." She asked her if she had an inventory. "What are you talking about now?"

"You said you were going to make me pay for it. I wondered how you were going to accomplish that if you didn't have an inventory of the shit that was in there. It's doubtful you'd get very much for any of it anyway. Is this all you wanted? For me to come down here so you could complain about your things being trashed?" Mom told her she wanted out. "Well, you should put your wants in one hand and your shit in the other and see which one of them gets attention faster. You should get something through your head right now, Mother. No one cares at all what you might want. Also, you need to get your head wrapped around the fact you're not ever getting out of here. Not upright, anyway. Neither is Phoenix. You've fucked up, and now you're caught. Deal with it."

"Who says? You? You might want to remember something, Amy. You're nothing either without me." Amy asked her how she'd come up with that. "I made your life what it is. You don't want to forget that. Without your sister and I opening doors for you in this world, you'd be nothing. Less than nothing. Don't think I've not heard about your little job. How much does it pay to have you go around taking pictures of kitties and pups?"

"Very well, as a matter of fact. My husband and I own a lovely home that is newly furnished. Our bank accounts are well stocked with billions of dollars of our money. You might say I've more money than I need." Mother told her that she lied. "No. That would be you that is the liar. You and Phoenix both. If there is nothing else, Mother dearest, I have to go and put Phoenix in her place. Too bad it's not in a body bag, but then I guess I can't hope everything goes my way."

She left her mom there, screaming at her to come back. Amy made her way down the hall, where she was told Phoenix was waiting for her. As soon as she entered the room on her crutches, Phoenix started complaining about not having enough to eat, not having her cell phone, and not having anything like the nice bed she had at home. Abby joined her in this room.

"Who the hell are you?" Abby told her who she was. "Like that means shit to me. I'm wanting to talk to my sister, not to some stranger from off the street. Is that why you're here? You're hoping my family will bail you out?

Don't count on it, girly. My family isn't going to part with anything until Mom and I say so."

"Is that what you think?" Amy felt like she was on a roll now. Not even bothering to curb her temper, she slammed her hands down on the table after storing her crutches against the wall. "Listen here, you overweight cock sucking bitch. You're not getting out. You're not going to be getting any special treatment. You will not be having Dad pay for an attorney. You and Mother have found your new home, so fucking get your heads out of your asses and make do with what you've got. I surely am going to enjoy every second you're not around to cause trouble. Lucky for you, the judge you shot didn't die. But she isn't going to be able to walk ever again, nor will she be able to feed herself or anything else that she could do before you stole a gun from an officer of the law and tried to shoot me. That was who you were aiming for, wasn't it? Your only sister?"

"Hell, yes, I was trying to put you out of my life. It would have been so much better had you not been born at all. Christ, I can't believe Mom didn't try and rid herself of you long before Dad found out about you." Amy asked her if she'd done that before. "How the fuck should I know? I'm her daughter, not her priest. But you're going to do a few things for me, and I don't want to hear shit about how you're not going to. I need some things brought to me so I can get by until I get out of here. You're going to do it, or so help me, I'll tell the world what sort of person you are."

"What sort of person am I, Phoenix? Do you even know? Tell me, what's my birthday? Month, day, and year? I know yours." Phoenix said she was full of shit. After rattling off the correct date for her sister's birthday, Phoenix asked her when she'd picked that up. "From you. Every year on your special week, you would tell me repeatedly as you knocked the shit out of me why you were able to do it. That being older than me by thirteen years gave you all sorts of rights I didn't have. Whatever they were, I certainly hope you enjoyed them. Because as of the moment you fired that gun, all specials of any sort were taken from you."

"So says you. Like I said, I want you to get some things for me from the house. I want you to make sure that I have my old bed back. This one here isn't fit for anyone." Abby got up and handed her her crutches. "Where the hell are you going? I want dates and times you'll be here with my things, Amy. I shit you not, I'm going to have things my way, or so help me, when I do get out, you're going to be toast."

"I like toast. You're not getting out, so I think I'm going to be all right without doing what you want." She was at the door when she turned back to her sister. "The funding you were getting from Dad is officially cut off. The things you had at the house are gone. There aren't going to be any visits from either of us. No money going to a good attorney to get you out. Frankly, Dad and I both like you right where you are. As for calling me again? Don't. As of the moment I walk out of this door, I'm finished with you and Mom both. Good luck in whatever lives you have coming to you. No one I know deserves it more than you two."

By the time she was in the lobby again, Amy had to sit down. Her leg was so shaky that she was sure she was going to collapse right there. Sitting down also had her crying. Saying things like that to anyone bothered her, but to have to talk to her mother and sister that way had hurt her deep in her heart and soul. Abby was there for her when she sobbed out how they'd hurt her, and how she didn't know what else to do.

"I'd say you did just what you needed to do. I didn't hear what you said to your mom, but the guards are talking about it all over. They said it was a come to Jesus meeting with you, and that you spared no punches in making sure she understood you were not going to take her shit. Did you?" Amy nodded at her friend. "Good for you. Now, if North can do the same to the other women in his family, we might have a good life after this. Did I tell you they're all going to trial as one unit? I heard this from Aiden just this morning. What the hell do they think they can accomplish by having a single trial for what they all did? I'd think they'd stand a better chance of some kind of life if they were tried separately. But what do I know? I'm just a pretty picture taker. One of them actually told their guard that's how I make a living, trying to keep Mars and I in food. Christ, I hate those women."

"I wish I had known Holly. She seems like such an amazing person for all the crap that happened to her." Abby told her she was. "North seems to have gotten his positive outlook on life from her. And Clayton is really coming around too. He and his brothers are dealing with a lot of shit they're finding out their wives were up to while they were married. I'm sorry for them at times."

"I was too for a while. But Mars pointed out that Holly never barred them from coming to see her. Any one of them at any time could have come to the correct information if they'd wanted to get the story straight. They are coming around, and I'm happy about it. But Mars wishes all the time that they'd gotten to know his mom like the rest of them had. She was the pillar of the family. More so than that old man that was her father." Amy asked her how she'd known Holly. "She saved my life a few times when I was growing up. Much like your family, mine was like that too. But my parents are both dead. Yours are still around, causing trouble. I lived with my uncle Lance for a long time. He used to be the funeral director in town. Boy, did he have a lot of stories."

"Thank you for this. I needed it." Abby told her she was there for her. "I can't thank you enough for everything you've done for me and North. This dinner tonight, it's going to be epic, I think. But it's also going to cause some tears. None of the fathers, I believe, have dealt firsthand with how much of an influence Holly did have on their sons' lives. This will be very telling for them."

"I never thought of that. She did influence them a great deal. I think she still is. But I believe you're right. This will be an eye-opener for them." As they traveled back to the house, she had Abby stop by the Village Posy Shop right on the main drag of their little town. She wanted to get North a dozen roses. "You know, that's a wonderful idea. Why do they get to be the ones that give roses? I'm going to do it too."

After getting them all flowers, they made their way back to her home. The furniture was being delivered, and there were extras helping them get it all inside. Even Mars, who still hadn't been able to move into their home, was helping. Abby was barred from even lifting the flowers she got for him.

Men were very odd when it came to women having babies. Amy decided she was going to tell them all she was going to have a baby someday while lifting weights with the due date written on them. She was reasonably sure North would have a stroke if they were to have a baby soon. She thought she'd just laugh at him.

Chapter 9

Wats had forgotten how much fun it was to cook. He'd been really busy the last few weeks and had only been having his meals at the hospital or at some fast-paced place. Tonight, he decided he was going to start cooking more. It was entirely relaxing.

Chopping vegetables. Cleaning the skins off cucumbers. All of it was like a well worked out play to him. Holly had told them all that timing was really everything. You didn't want to have your toast finished up while you were still waiting to fry the bacon. Things had to come together in a timely fashion, or you had limp toast and underdone meat.

"Did you know you can buy carrots and other things like onions already chopped up?" He asked Shawn if he was serious. "I am. When I went by the store to pick up more carrots for tonight, there were containers full of chopped up things. Celery of all things. Chopped up like it's not one of the easiest things in the world to cut into pieces."

"I could be tempted to buy cut up onions. I mean, I hate having my hands smell like onions for days afterward." Mars told him all he had to do was to wash up with a lemon. "Does that work?"

They were all giving advice on things they'd picked up here and there. Mars said Abby had told him about the lemons. Then to put the citrusy thing in the garbage disposal to make it fresh. Wats wondered aloud what their aunt would say about them cooking for their dads today.

"She'd be in there with them telling them they're lazy and should have learned to cook too." They all laughed with Booker. "Yesterday I was thinking about some of the things Aunt Holly would tell us about one of her brothers. I have to be honest and tell you I was sure she was making things up about them just to make us not completely write them off. But the more I get to know my own dad, I can see she was telling us the truth. It's like seeing my dad in different eyes—through her eyes, if you want to know the truth."

Just as they were talking about other things Aunt Holly had said, his dad and the others came into the room with them. It was Clayton, North's dad, who asked them to tell them things about their sister. It had been like that for the last few days with him and his dad. He would ask for stories about her so that they, he supposed, in some way, could feel connected with her again.

"She loved the holidays. Not just the traditional ones, but anything and everything that was written on a calendar." North laughed as he continued. "Aunt Holly used to tell us if someone took the time to write it on the calendar, then it was our duty to celebrate it. I think her favorite one was Halloween."

"Yes, next to Christmas." Everyone agreed with him on that one. "When we were hanging around with her, we never really participated in dressing up and going out. I think mostly it was because we were terrified that if one of our mothers' so-called friends would tell on us, we'd never be able to do things with her again. But each year, she would have a theme for Halloween. The one I remember the best was when she had us all dress up like the cast to that under the sea cartoon. She even had us all costumes to wear."

"That's my favorite too. They were good costumes too. I was Patrick." His cousins were laughing with Brandon when he spoke up. "She would even have things to give away at the door that were a part of the theme. All the kids would flock to her home. She didn't cheapen the candy she gave out either. It was full-sized candy bars. Each of us would talk to the kids coming to the house. Aunt Holly took pictures too."

"I have them." When Mars went to get the albums, Wats waited for the rest of his story until Mars returned. "Here they are. I was thinking about this the other day, how she would add a picture of all of us dressed up to her albums, and dug this one out."

"She made everything seem like a game. Like teaching

us to cook." Wats thought about telling them how he'd been knocked around once, and she'd taught him how to make a New York style cheesecake, but he didn't want to bring the room down. "Each visit with her was an adventure. She never demanded anything of us but to not talk about our parents. Unless it was in a good light."

"I'm doubting there were many conversations about us then." His dad looked sad about his comment. It was difficult on him, Wats knew, to find out things that had been kept from him. Not so much as kept from him, but that he'd not wanted to know. Wats thought all the dads were having that trouble. It was North that had Dad smiling again, telling him how she always told them about growing up with five older brothers. "She wasn't your typical little girl. You guys know that, don't you? She was just as much into things as we were as youngsters."

"She wasn't perfect. Not the way we make her sound." They all turned to Mars when he spoke from his position at the stove. "Once when I was seventeen, Mom got written up at work for telling one of the people she worked with off. But when she realized she had been wrong about it, or anything for that matter, Mom would be the first person to say she was sorry about it. The one thing I remember her teaching all of us was that once you start to think of yourself as a perfect being, that was when someone out there would take you down a peg or two. It wasn't until I was older that I realized she meant her own dad. I think it hurt her the most that he'd turned his back on her."

"Aunt Holly would tell me often that I was her knight in shining armor when she was down about something. She worked hard too, and made sure we all understood the value of being a responsible person." Wats remembered one such conversation with his aunt that he thought of to this day. "When I turned sixteen, all I wanted was a car of my own to drive back and forth to school. It was the thing to do—be a driver, not a rider. When I went to her complaining about how I'd not gotten what I wanted, she smacked me, really hard. It was then she asked me if I wanted to be a man or a shit. I was hurt, so I told her I wanted to be a shit."

"Why did she hit you?" Wats smiled at his dad when he asked. "I don't know that I'm going to like this answer, am I?"

"I know, for a very long time, I didn't like her answer either. Nodding at my answer, she just went about cooking dinner for the three of us—her, Mars, and I. Nothing more was mentioned about it until we were cleaning up. She told me I could just go to the living room and watch television while she and Mars cleaned up. While I was in there, enjoying the break from having to do chores, I could hear her and Mars in the kitchen laughing. Having fun, as we always do when we're together. As soon as I entered the kitchen off and on while they worked, they'd shut up and tell me to go watch television. That was when I realized I was being a shit, and she was treating me like one. A shit that didn't care if others had to work hard to give me something I wanted. The break from doing the dishes and not helping — she was showing me how shits would act."

"I don't get it." Dad looked at the others, and they didn't seem to understand either. "She just let you have the evening off from chores. How is that teaching you a lesson?"

"She was telling him if he wanted a car, he should make it so he could have one. Find himself a job, save his money, and buy it on his own." Dad understood but still seemed confused. Mars explained. "Mom thought that all of us, coming from money, needed to learn the value of things. Not just have them handed to us on a platter. Having him sit in the other room while the two of us worked was giving him a break, sure, but he was missing out on all the other things that came with working. We were having fun. Wats might well have too, except for the fact he wanted someone to do the job — in this case, clean up while he did nothing at all."

"Eight months later, I'd saved up enough to buy a secondhand car and was more proud of it than I was of anything I'd ever gotten handed to me. She not only took good care of us, but she taught us things like working for something, as well as appreciating what you have by sharing with those that have nothing. That was another thing she wanted us to learn. Sharing." Dad asked him if he still had his car. "I do. So does Booker and the rest of us. Mars, I don't think he had his own car until he graduated from college. North bought himself his first new vehicle just recently."

"I miss her." Dad looked around the room at the others. "I know it's our fault for cutting her out of our lives. I know had we done anything at all, she would still be alive and giving us a hard time about this or that. I know all that. But what my head knows and my heart feels are two entirely different things. I miss her so much every day, boys. Just having you guys around, telling us stories about your lives with her? It's all I can do not to find myself a nice dark corner and sob for all we've lost."

"But, you've lost nothing." Abby stood in the doorway with Amy when she spoke. "Don't you see? You've lost nothing by her being gone. I know it hurts you. Christ, I miss her very much too. But you have to remember this. If she'd not been cut from your lives when she was if she'd not had the relationship with your sons, do you think any of this would be happening? Do you think you would have been any happier with your wives the way they are? No. Would you have still had your sons? I doubt that either. You have to think of her being gone like this. Without the chain of events the way they were, none of this—not your families, your lives, none of it—would have been possible. You are who you are because of what formed you. Holly formed a relationship with your boys because they needed her as much as she did them. What do you think would have happened if things had been perfect? Not this, that's for sure. At least that's the way I think of her being gone. She was and still is the catalyst that has made you all who you are. And who you will be in the future. Holly Wilkerson is the reason for the events that made this meal happen too."

Wats kissed Abby on the cheek. She had it right. Aunt Holly, if she'd been here today, would have kicked all their asses for being so sad about things they had no control over. She was murdered, but before she was, Aunt Holly had given the cousins all she could have been giving her brothers. This, Wats thought, was the way it should have been. Just the way it had to be to work out in the way that made them come together once again.

The meal was a huge success, so much so they decided they wanted to do this more often, getting together as a family and cooking a huge meal to share. They talked about everything yet nothing at all. They laughed at the expense of others without being cruel. Laughter rang loudly between them. Sorrow too. By the time they were having pie and homemade ice cream, thanks to the two wives, each of them were groaning about how they'd never eat again, that they'd eaten too much. Wats was sure they had. There were no leftovers.

Clean up took longer than he thought it should have because they were deciding things, major things, like which part of the meal was the best, who had made what part of it, and when would they do it again.

Wats would never forget this night. Nor for so long as he lived would he forget the look on his dad's face when he bit down on his mashed potatoes with white gravy.

He'd always remember Uncle Hank's face when he sipped the first sip of his tea and declared it better than his own mother's. Wats watched as each of them helped set and break down the table, and knew the moment Uncle Wesley realized they were using a sheet as a tablecloth because no one had remembered to get one. Things like that, little things as well as larger ones, would come back to him, he knew, at the oddest times. Just as things he had learned at the home of the most courageous woman he'd ever know.

Holly Wilkerson. Mother to them all, friend too. Wats found himself walking away for a moment, just to gather his own emotions. He realized he was never going to get a hug from her again. That she was gone from his and the others' lives forever. Wats thought his heart was breaking all over when he thought of how much she was missing this day. Wats loved her so much, he wondered if he'd ever find someone to love as much as she did all of them.

~*~

Clayton was as ready as he'd ever been. In the past, when his wife would speak at him, not to him, he would barely listen to her. Knowing she would remind him several times of something he'd have to do so he'd not forget anything. Agreeing with her, all of them was easier than trying to change her mind about anything going on. It wasn't always right if it was easy, he was beginning to understand.

Today, he decided, as the oldest male in the family, he was going to set his foot down and make sure these women knew what was what. Clayton glanced over at Amy. She was going to be his ass-kicker if he needed a boost. Not to the wives, she'd explained to him, but to *his* ass. Clayton was a little intimidated by his beautiful daughter-in-law.

He felt renewed since last night. Like, instead of just going along with whatever the women told him, he was going to be the one that held the conversation. There would be no more just going along with things simply because he didn't want to deal with it. He'd done that for far too long, and he'd lost his sister and his father because of his lack of being a man. That was another thing that had been pointed out to him by Amy just last night after dinner. He'd been less than a man, and it had nearly cost him his son.

"You fuck up this time, and not only will you lose out big time, but Clayton, you might well miss out on having grandchildren that want to visit you. Or even to be seen with you. I shit you not. You fuck this up, and there will be hell to pay. Not only are your brothers depending on you right now, but you could say the entire Wilkerson lineage." He nodded, then shook his head. "I don't understand. You want to fuck this up?"

"No. No, not that. But I don't care about how my brothers are depending on me. Nor about the lineage of my family. It could all go to hell for all I care about those things. I feel I have to do this for my son. The rest? Well, they can come here and do this better if they think they can. I want my son to finally realize his father is someone that will now and forever forward be someone he can depend on. I need this for him." Amy got up, and he was sure she was crying, but when she wrapped her arms around him, hugging him like she'd never done before, Clayton hugged her tightly back. "You did this for us, Amy. This thing with my son. I was just beginning to break through with some sort of progress, but after you showed up, it was like I became what I should have been all along."

So now here he was today, standing in a room that would soon be filled with women that not only killed his wife but his sister, and had destroyed any sort of relationship he could have had with his son when he'd been younger. He had his notes to go over. Points he wanted to be assured they understood. Mostly, he thought, it was to finally get them out of their lives once and for all time.

As soon as they were brought into the room and locked down, Clayton felt the weight of their eyes on him, just as he did when he'd been married to the ring leader of them all. Bracing himself for whatever they said, it was the most difficult thing he thought he'd ever done. Be a man. Who would have thought it would take him till so late in his life to grow a set of balls again?

"So? What the fuck do you want, Clayton? And what in the holy name of Christ are you wearing? You are never to come here again, looking like that. Do I make myself clear?" He looked down at his jeans and tennis shoes. He'd forgotten he was wearing them, they'd been so comfy. "And I do hope you've moved out of the house. As soon as I'm out of here, Wesley and I will be moving in and running things. Also, you'd better be working on getting that piece of shit Mars out of our lives. I swear to you if he's still around—"

"Shut the fuck up." Tina looked at him. It almost took him back to a time when he was afraid of them all when Amy cleared her throat. That was all, she cleared her throat, and he felt himself ready again. "You murdering bunch of bitches are not getting out of here. I don't have any idea why you would even assume that you would. The lot of you conspired and killed my baby sister for no other reason than jealously. She was only a child, a little girl, and you sold her off to be raped and murdered. But she was so much better than any of you. Even when she knew, she knew all along, that you were the ones that had done this to her, she never once said a bad word against any of you. She raised our sons to be good, powerful men that have more heart than any of you would ever have."

"Are you finished?" He looked at Christa, Josiah's wife, and asked her what she had to say. "We will be getting out of here because we're going to have a long conversation with your brothers, and they're going to spend whatever it will cost for us to get out of here. We rule the roost, Clayton, and the sooner you remember that, the longer you might be around to watch us keep the Wilkersons as pure as they were when your dad was still around, God rest his soul."

"Mars and his wife are going to have a baby soon. Now that North is married, I'm sure that soon enough, he'll be having children too. And you want to know what,

Christa? I could care less if they were half Wilkerson and half moonstone." He felt his face heat up when he realized what he'd said, but continued. "I have moved out of the big house. Right now, it's being totally revamped and updated. All the furniture in the home has been sold off and replaced with things that are comfortable and easy to take a nap in. You know who's going to be living in it? Mars and his wife. They're having the entire house stripped out and starting over. It was a mess in there. I cannot believe that in all the years, no one mentioned how dirty and black it was. Well, it'll be filled with laughter. Have bright rooms with children laughing and having fun in the yard. Christmases that don't make you feel as if you're in a cave without lights are fun."

When Penelope started to speak, Amy told her to shut up, calling her Penny, a name that he knew she detested. As soon as her mouth closed, Tina snickered. He watched in astonished horror as the two women started snarling at each other like a pack of wolves. Clayton looked at Amy.

"That's what they are, you know. Animals." He nodded, watching the guards separate them as they began name-calling, spitting on each other. Clayton took a step back when he realized this wasn't the first time he'd seen them like this.

"They've been animals their entire life. My wife, she was one of them too." Amy asked him if he'd been hurt by any of them. He looked at her. "Yes. Not just physically, but many times verbally. I've only just realized they have never been right in the head. My coming here today with you? It's useless, isn't it?"

"I would say so."

He continued to watch as the guards finally pulled out their Tasers to use on the four of them. It only seemed to serve to make them angrier, to piss them off to the point where they were now as one against the guards.

Amy went on. "The only way to take care of a wild animal is to put it down. I think—and since I'm only an in-law, you can take this or leave it—but I don't think there is a thing you could say to any of them that they want to hear. And so long as they don't want to hear it, they'll never come to terms with anything you say to them."

"They were always like this. Even my father, he would just go along with them rather than to get them to this point. So that their madness, their lack of restraint, came through. Christ, how did this get by all of us for so long? I know the answer to that, I guess. We all found it easier to do what they said rather than to be confronted by this. Oh, Amy, I can't imagine my son going through this now. How on earth did I let him be hurt like this?" Amy asked him if he was ready to go. "I am. I won't be back. I want to do just what you did with your mother and sister. Cut them out of my life and be done with them all. I've no reason whatsoever to ever return here."

"I'd not go to the trial unless you're there to testify. I know you will at some point, but I'd only show up then. Or work out something with your attorney so that you can do it from a remote place. It's not worth you getting stressed out about them any longer."

Clayton raised his face to the sunshine when they were out of the prison. He wondered how even the people working there could stand the way it was so closed up.

"You're a good man, Clayton. I wanted to tell you that. Also, you should be aware that North loves you. Loves spending time with you and having you around now. You were very lucky in that your sister made them into the men you can be proud of."

"I am a lucky man. I know that more than ever now." He turned and looked at her. "I have a feeling you were to come with me to take over if I failed, weren't you?" Amy laughed, telling him he was wrong. "Then, why are you here today? I'm sure you could have been doing a million and one things rather than being here with me trying to make four crazy women listen to me."

"No. I wanted to spend time with you today. I didn't care to come here; I'll be honest with you. But just hanging out with you, getting to know the real man you are, was all I had plans for. I never thought you'd fuck up too much." They both laughed. "As I said to North before we left, you would have made Holly very proud of you. She would have been extremely proud of all her brothers."

As they were driving back to town, he thought of what she'd said to him and what was said last night. Would she have been proud of him? Clayton decided he wanted that. More than anything. But something else came to his mind as he drove.

"My sister wouldn't want us to keep bringing up what we lost with her being gone." Amy said she didn't know Holly, but thought he might be right. "Yes. I do believe I am. She's gone, and while we won't ever forget her, we don't have to compare our lives to what it might have been had she been here. I think I'm going to work on not dwelling on the past and what we lost, but the future and what might come. Like grandchildren."

Amy laughed. "Yes, well, I don't know what our plans are for children, to be honest. Right now, we're working hard at just getting to know each other. Getting our lives back on track. I think North is loving taking cases that he wants to take. And being able to work with you and his uncles. I'm unable to take pictures right now, but it's been a lot of fun working with Abby in the studio that she and I are going to have together."

"What about your mom and sister?" She shrugged, and he told her he was sorry for bringing them up. "Don't be. They're a part of what we're getting on track with as well. I want to tell you they don't matter to me anymore, but that wouldn't be the truth. I'd love to tell you I've washed my hands of them both, but that would also be a lie. I'm their sister and daughter, no matter how much I'd like to think on the contrary."

"North told me you've changed your phone number and fired the staff you hired from amongst the staff at one of the houses." She told him how the butler was giving the women information about them when he visited them. "I guess that happened a great deal too. I'm going to do that as well. I might even tell my brothers to do the same. But I think we all need to learn a new way of living. To stop looking to the past for answers when we need to be making our future into what we can. I'm sick of being sad all the time for things I feel I lost. I'm going to start living like a man again. Hell, I might even find someone to date."

"You might want to think about getting laid too. I bet it's been a lot longer than you remember." He didn't ask, but he was sure no one currently working for them would side with the women. Also, he thought he was going to take her advice on getting laid. It had been way too long. "Also, I know you like living in the condo and are enjoying just being by yourself at times. There will always be room for you should you want to come and stay with us. As I said, I don't know about grandchildren right now, but I do expect you to be in their lives as much as you want."

"I want to be as much a part of their lives as I can. Yours and North's as well." She said she'd like that too. "Good. Amy, I would like to ask you a favor. I want you to...not hit me too terribly hard, but when you see me getting all emotional, just shake me up a little. Get me moving in the right direction."

"I promise I won't hurt you too much, but you're right, Clayton, it is time for all of you to move. Even North and the others. Whichever way you want, but you really do need to start moving." She laughed, and he asked her what she thought was so funny. "You should run for mayor. From what I've heard about this one, he's a jackass. I think there has been some shady business going on that needs to be taken care of. When I saw that elections were coming up, you're the first person I thought of. You'd do a great job. And knowing the law would be an added advantage over this jerk because you'd follow them instead of bending the shit out of them."

He thought about it off and on all the way home. Clayton also thought about how he was going to be moving on. Loving his sister was all he'd ever do, but it was time for him to stop thinking about how he'd missed so much and begin to make memories for him and his family while he still had them. Yes, he thought, it was time to get to living again.

Chapter 10

North hung up the phone and sat there for several minutes. Lorinda had died. Charlie had called him first, telling him her mom had requested at some point in her life for no one to do anything heroic to save her.

"Mom told me a few weeks ago, when I was visiting with her, that she was a believer in donating organs. That I was to, if I could, make sure she didn't lie around rotting her organs when someone else could use them." Charlie cried then, telling him something he'd not known about the woman. "I'm doing that now. Making sure someone else has a chance at life even if hers was snuffed out too young."

"I'm so sorry. I really respected her." She told him that she had him as well. "Thank you for that. I wouldn't have become an attorney without her there pushing me to be the best. Your mom, she sure could be a mean bitch when she wanted."

Charlie laughed with him. "She's the reason I'm not

an attorney. I wanted to be one, don't get me wrong, but she told me there was no middle ground in being one. You either loved it or hated it. I think toward the end, she didn't care for it much." North had known that as well. She'd told him many times she wished she'd been a doctor instead. He asked Charlie what she was going to do now. "Go to her home. Get rid of whatever I don't want and move on. It would have pissed her off to no end if I sat around being depressed about losing her."

"It would have at that. I can almost hear her now. Telling you to get up off your ass and get to work at cleaning out shit for her." Charlie laughed, which he supposed he'd wanted her to do. "What will you tell the rest of them? She had a sister, didn't she?"

"Aunt Rose. I don't think I'll tell her at all. Aunt Rose has been in a nursing home for the last few years. She had a stroke and never fully recovered from it." North told her again he was sorry. "No reason to be, North. Aunt Rose was a hellcat when she was younger. Mom used to say that Rose was getting some much needed rest now. She sure didn't have much when she was growing up. Aunt Rose is about twelve years older than Mom anyway. I don't think they were very close."

After telling her he'd be there for her if she needed it, they hung up. North wondered what would happen to Lorinda's seat now. It would be very difficult filling her spot as a sitting judge. There was no one like her—fair, but firm and funny, and serious too. She was going to be a hell of an act to follow.

When his phone rang again, he nearly didn't answer it. But when he saw it was his dad, he picked it up, smiling. He wanted to hear firsthand what happened at the jail today. He'd heard a little from Amy when she got back, but her ankle was bothering her, and she had to lie down for a little bit.

"I'm done talking about them. From now on, son, we're only going to talk about the here and now. What do you say?" He agreed with him. "Good. Okay, I need your help. That little missus of yours put a bug in my ear today, and I'm going to do it, by golly. I'm going to run for mayor."

"Really?" Dad laughed and said he was as good as if not better than the idiot they had now. "That's very true. I heard yesterday that he's going to be running on the same ticket he did the last time and did nothing about. I think he was going to bring in more businesses. Dad, your family alone has done that without even trying."

"That's right." Dad laughed. "I also want to move in with you and that little girl of yours. She set me straight on things there too. I'll tell you about them later. I love her, North. I know you do, but so do I. She's just the ticket I need for being a man again. Would you believe it, she told me to get laid."

"Not what I want to think about when I'm thinking of you." Dad laughed, and North couldn't help but join him. "All right. So you're running for mayor and getting laid. Is there anything else I should know about?"

"Yes. One thing. I should have said this more often. I love you, North. I love you more than I ever thought it was possible to love your own flesh and blood." North felt his heart tighten in his chest. He couldn't remember his father ever saying that to him. "You're the best thing that has ever happened to me, and I plan, for the rest of my life, to be with you as much as you'll allow it. I'm going to be the best damned grandda that has ever been made too. You watch and see."

"I believe you, Dad. And I love you too." They both were silent then, working, North was sure, on being manly instead of babbling like a fool. "You move in with us, and it will make me the happiest man in the world. With you and Shelton here, it'll be the best home any of us have ever lived in."

"You betcha. I do want to tell you that my new style was as much a hit as I thought it would be. To be honest, I'd forgotten I was wearing them when one of the women pointed out how bad I looked. Could have died a happy man right then and there. I won't, not for a long time if I can help it." Dad laughed. "Before I forget, I'm going to change my phone number. I might need your help in doing that. I told the prison I don't want any more calls from them unless it's to make funeral arrangements. And even then, I might just tell them to plant her in the back yard. I tell you, son, this living thing is pretty heady stuff, isn't it?"

"It is. I think you're doing a good job of it too."

Forgetting for the moment his pain of losing his friend while speaking with his dad, North believed his dad had it right. To forget the past and start living with the now. He thought about seeing Amy large with his child. It was all he could do not to hang up on his dad and go talk to her about having a child of their own. "Dad, it's maybe too soon, but what do you want to do about the things in the house you took? Mom's jewelry? There were, I think, some paintings you took too. Amy has looked them over, and I think she said it wouldn't take long to clean them up. She said they were dusty more than dirty."

That had been a surprise to him too. That even though his father had lived in the house that Mars was making his own, there were lots of rooms he'd never stepped foot in. Dad and Mars were finding all sorts of things Dad didn't know about.

"I'm going to sell it all. Unless it's family stuff, then we'll keep it. But with her things—and from what I've remembered from the inventory from the police, there was a great deal of it—we'll have ourselves a garage sale and donate what doesn't sell. Surely there are others out there who could use some of that stuff." North loved this newer version of his dad. "Also, I've got it in my head that when I do move in, I'm going to need myself a car. And a driver's license. I've not driven in longer than I care to remember. I might enjoy that."

"I love to drive. Taking the car around for special occasions makes it feel like it is special. I can take you to the motor vehicles office soon. Also, if you want to look at cars, that's good too. I need to get Amy one when she's able to drive again." Dad asked when he could start moving things to the house. "Anytime. As you know, there are quite a few bedrooms that are still empty. Shelton, he lives on the second floor. I think he was planning to be there when the children arrive."

"I like that idea. We can each take an end." Dad was as excited as he'd ever heard him sound. North decided to take his idea and run with it too. Being down about everything was very wearing. "North, do you think us working together is going to be all right? I have to tell you, it's been fun for me. Getting to know the law again. Digging into a case or two. Even my brothers have been having some fun when we get together. It's been like a family project for us to see what we can use when I have a case."

"I'm looking forward to it, Dad. And as you said earlier, there is enough space between us that if we have some conflict, we can cool off in our own area." So far, that hadn't been an issue. Dad had been working from home for the last couple of days, working up to the talk at the prison. "I'm looking forward to having both you and Shelton living here. Perhaps the two of you can do things together too. He's a good man."

"He and I have been comparing notes on life. That'll have to change too. I'll have him looking at life like I have. Seeing the future." Dad laughed. "Son, I love you. I have to get going now. I have things to do. I want some ugly sheets. Ones that have the most god-awful designs on them, so I wake up with a smile. I'm never going to have a white silk sheet on my bed for any kind of money. I want good old fashioned cotton, damn it."

When his dad hung up, North sat there smiling for a while. His dad was right. There had to be more to life than white silk sheets all the time. Getting up from his desk where he'd only been looking over contracts for the businesses that Amy owned, he decided to go and find his old bike. It had to be around someplace. He thought perhaps it was still in the garage at the big house. North decided to walk there.

It never occurred to him that walking would have been so enlightening. He talked with people walking along the sidewalk. Made a friend of the dog that sat outside the gas station that also had the oldest looking pop machine he'd ever seen. As he was making his way toward where Mars was working on his business, Wilkerson Pharmaceutical, he found the candy machines Mars was going to have in the place.

"I'm going to make this a fun place to be while you might have to wait a little longer on things. Did I tell you my first shipment of drugs came in with an armed guard? It was more fun signing off on it than I've had in a while." North sat in one of the many booths that were going to be for the ice cream shoppe renting space from Mars to do business. Mars joined him. "Amy was in earlier. She was telling me about a photoshoot she wants to arrange in my back yard. I told her so long as no one knew where she was taking the pictures, then to go for it. I had no idea that some of the plants and flowers back there were rare."

"She was thinking about asking you to use it for engagement photos. But after speaking to Abby, she decided that it was a terrible idea. They didn't want someone looking for a way to get into the house. They would, too, I think." Mars sat down next to him in the booth. "My dad and I just spoke. He's going to forget the sorrow of the past and start living for the now. As much as I'd like to do that too, I think it'll be hard on him just a little until this aunt thing is over with. I hope not, but I don't think he's going to be able to just ignore it."

"I do." North asked him why he thought that. "Like your dad, I don't care. I've come to the conclusion that I can't bring my mom back by hating these women. I don't like them, that's a given, but I'm not going to waste any more time of my life wondering when they're getting out. From what I've been told, they're not."

"You think you can do that? I hope we all can." Mars smiled. He told him he had a baby coming. "I know that, dork. What does that have to do with this?"

"Everything. Like I said, wasting my energy worrying about them when I could be spending it with my child is going to stop. I'm going to devote my life to being happy. A good father and a better cousin to you guys than I have always been." North said that he'd been the best. "Thank you. But I'm going to be better. I'm not trying to be a smart ass here, but I want to be better at everything I do. Also, I'm going to enjoy life to the fullest. Abby and I are looking at traveling. Buying one of those big campers with all the amenities of home and seeing the seven wonders of the country. You know which ones I mean. The largest ball of string, like my mom wanted to go see."

"That does sound like fun. I can't remember the last time I had a vacation that didn't involve working a little on the side. Now with a wife and hopefully a family soon, I can make myself take some time off and do just that." He asked him about the camper. "Are you really going to get one of those bigger ones?"

"I am. I don't know crap about camping or even how to set one up, but if I'm going to do it, I'm going to make sure I'm comfortable while I'm learning. Remember when you and I were going to go out west and see the Corn Palace? Then we looked it up. It's a building with corn all over it. I am going to go see that. Just because I can."

They were both laughing when Mars was called away for another delivery. North looked out the front of the building to the street beyond. He thought of how much fun it would be to come here on his lunch hour. Mars had already decided he was going to have a lunch menu from eleven to two. Abby was going to do the cooking, as she'd decided quite recently that she'd rather stay home and take her pictures than to travel. Especially with a baby coming.

"Hey there, young man. Are you Mr. Wilkerson?

North Wilkerson?" The elderly man sat down across from him and smiled when North told him that was who he was. "My name is James Oliver. I live on the little farm you recently purchased."

"Yes. I remember now. I'm so sorry, I forgot to go and see you. I've only recently gotten married too." Mr. Oliver told him it was just fine. He'd been a little under the weather. "I'm sorry to hear that. As I said, I've been meaning to go over and talk to you. How are you doing with the house there?"

"I'm just fine. Just fine. I have me a little garden there that I've— Well, I'm sure you don't want to hear that." North told him he did want to hear it. "All right then. I've put me in a little garden this year. I have tomatoes that I love. Some green beans too. Did you know you can have just a veggie meal and feel quite satisfied? I do, anyway. But I was coming to talk to you about a couple of things. The banker that was holding my rent, he was never a good one to get in to talk to about stuff. I know I'm a bit behind on my rent, but I'm working on it. Selling a few of the things I can't eat from the garden is helping me a bit."

"Mr. Oliver, I'm to understand you've lived in that house there for a number of years." He told him he'd been there twenty-three years. "That's a good long time to rent from someone. What are you paying for rent there? I'm sure between the two of us, we can work out something that will help you along."

"I'm paying for my wife's funeral, you see. The new

place they wanted more money a month than I could do. Mr. Farley, he was a good man, nice fella, but this new man, he wants things done up now." North said he'd forgotten about the sale of the funeral home. "Wish it didn't happen, but I know things gotta change. Anywho, I've been trying to catch up. I want you to know that. But it's been a little hard on me with no income much to speak of. My retirement money from the school has been cut back a couple of times lately, and it's been hard to make ends meet anywhere close to the middle."

Mr. Oliver turned away and wiped at his face. Mars came to sit with him again and handed him a sheet of paper. On it was things that Mr. Oliver had been telling him, also that the bank was still owed three months of back rent. Then it asked if he could help him.

"Mr. Oliver, I'm not going to charge you rent for living in the house. As far as I'm concerned, anyone living in a place for as long as you have should be able to live out the rest of his days without having to wonder whether he should eat or pay the rent. My wife and I, we'd like for you to use the money you were paying us to make things just a little better for yourself." The older man looked at him with so much hope that North wished he'd gone to see him sooner. "Also, if you'd not mind. I'm going to have a crew go out there and see if we can fix some of the things that might need a little tweaking."

"There is a nice hole in the roof. But as I said, the banker, he didn't think fixing it was worth the money."

North decided to find the banker and have a talk with him about people and their needs. "I'm sorry. I didn't come here to make you give me a place to live. I just wanted to make sure you understood that I'm not a freeloader."

"Of course, you're not. I never once thought that." Mr. Oliver thanked him. "No need for that. The place should have been taken care of long before now. I'm in a position to take care of it, and I will. You'll have a nicer home even if we have to build you a new one."

"No, that won't be necessary. My granddaughter, Rayne, is coming to visit me soon. I think she'll be going to college from my home for a bit. It would be nice to have the roof fixed before she comes. But the other stuff, it's not necessary."

But it was. Not only to North, but it seemed to Mars as well. When Mr. Oliver left them a bit later, Mars asked him if he could help with the home.

"I'm sure you will be helping me, but for now, I want to have someone go out and inspect the house. I have a feeling more than the big hole in the roof is wrong with it." Mars told him he had someone that could do that for him. "I'm sure you do. You're a very resourceful man. But I think I just want to have him a home put out there, but make sure it's going to be feasible. He's more than paid for it, I think, for renting the place for so many years."

Mars agreed. When they had settled how to get him a house put on the property, thanks a great deal to their wives, the two of them decided to take the walk that

North had started together. The town, they knew, needed someone to see it through some things. North told Mars that his dad was running for mayor.

"He'd be really good at it, I think." North agreed with him. "This walk, is it for his benefit for yours? You're not going to run against your father, are you?"

"Goodness no. But it only started out as just a walk. I haven't been around town in a while. By the way, your house is looking like it should have a long time ago. Planting those flowering bushes out front did make a difference to how welcoming it is.

He and Mars had been the best of friends growing up. It hadn't changed that much since they were both adults. The only difference North noticed was that Mars seemed more relaxed like he'd been when they were both younger. He supposed it was just knowing he didn't have to worry about things. It had helped him and his stress levels too.

"I'm glad you came by today. I've been meaning to ask you about a couple of things. And by all means, you can tell me no if you want. But I'd like to continue some of the traditions my mom had. Not necessarily dressing up at Halloween like we used to, but to be at the condo to hand out candy together." North said he'd like that. "Good. The second thing. I'd very much like to be able to host family holidays together. In the big house. Not like your parents had, stuffy people, paying too much to have the privilege of having a snack in the house. I want it to be family. Also, actual friends. Again, not like it was."

"Amy and I were talking about that just the other day. She's never really had a celebration of Christmas and Thanksgiving. I'm assuming those are the family holidays you're talking about." Mars said they were. "I think it would be great for all of us. I don't think I've even been to the big house since my mom was killed. I know you're renovating it, and it's coming along, but I don't know the last time I was in it before that."

"I'm enjoying the plans that are going on. I didn't think I would at first. But finding things in the house, things that my mom told me about, certainly makes it easier for me to stay there." He smiled. "I even had myself a slide down the old banister before they replaced it."

They ended up walking to his home. Mars had money, much more than he thought anyone in the world would have had. And he was using it. There were so many crews working on the house that he thought it should be done before too much longer. North asked Mars about it.

"Yes. By the end of the month. Only two weeks from now. I'm walking around looking at what they're doing, and I can't help but think someone is a little overzealous about how much they can get done. But really, all the major things are finishing up. It doesn't look like a constant construction zone anymore." They looked at the main hall, a place that had foretold how dark the house was going to be before Mars had it brightened with new wallpaper and a beautiful chandelier. "Most of the stuff we're using was stored in the big barn out back. This thing here weighs a ton but looks better than those ugly lights that were in there when we started this project. Same for the lighting in the library and the dining room."

North loved the new and improved house. The entrance hall alone was better than he'd ever seen it. The living room had been a place he'd never been in much. However, now that it was finished up, North could see having holidays in here just as Mars wanted. He asked if he'd run across his bike while rummaging through the barn. Mars laughed.

"I nearly had it bronzed for you. I remember you riding that thing to our house and hiding it in the garage so no one would find you there. But once I started looking at it, North, I realized it was in terrible shape. Rusty, and the tires were all rotted. You'd be better off getting you something newer. That way, I won't have to worry about you getting something from it while riding around." They were both laughing as they entered the kitchen. "This is what Abby wanted. It's all her design."

The kitchen was a chef's dream, North thought. While there seemed to be a lot of equipment, there didn't seem to be a clutter. The counter held a mixer, oversized at that, a tea maker, as well as some things he didn't have a name for. North asked him when the room would be finished.

"That is debatable." He laughed. "Abby has been cooking in here since we moved in last week. Every time she does, the workers moan. She finds something else that isn't what she needs. Last weekend, she decided the refrigerator was much too small. So, that was changed out. This is an ongoing process. The workers are saying done just about the time Abby finds something else to change."

The two of them left the house in favor of continuing their walk. North especially enjoyed it because he was seeing the town in a different light than he ever had before. He'd always had a fear of his mom finding him doing something in town and knocking him around a bit. North figured since they were out and about, he'd take notes on things his dad could add to his campaign. It was going to be great having him as mayor.

Heading back to his home later that afternoon, North had a long list of things he'd noticed that needed to be taken care of. Mostly it was broken sidewalks in front of shops. But there were things he thought needed immediate attention like the tree that had been lying across the parking lot of the nearby retirement village. Both he and Mars had spoken to some of the people living there.

"The tree fell almost two years ago this month. I swear, it's like pulling teeth to talk to the mayor about it. All he does is tell us he's cutting his budget as close as he can. I don't believe that for a minute." Mrs. Sawyer huffed at Mars when he asked her if he could send a crew out. "Will they show? The last time I was told that it was six months before someone came out. Even then, they told us they didn't have the right equipment. I'm an eighty-four-year-old woman, and I can see what sort of equipment it takes. You get me a chainsaw, Mars, and I'll cut the sucker up all by myself. What is wrong with people these days? I tell you what's wrong. They're lazy as my old cat was. Wouldn't even catch a mouse in favor of lying in the sun. I fixed his ass up, I did. I put him out on the porch and off my sofa, and that surely changed his mind."

North called his foreman at the house and told him what he needed. In less than five minutes, six men were working on the tree and removing it. Mrs. Sawyer gave them all two dollars for helping an old woman out.

"Now. You want to have that daddy of yours be mayor, you tell him to come and see me. I'll give him some things that he can use for his campaign." North told her he'd do that. "You tell that daddy of yours, he'd better be nice to me. I have two kinds of chocolate chip cookies at my place, for those that do and those that don't. He don't want to be on the don't list. Them cookies are older than snot and have some of them chips they use for a laxative. I'll surely feed them to him if he makes me upset. I don't like being upset either."

"No, I can see you'd not like that." North didn't look at Mars. The expression on his face was enough to have him hurting to laugh. "I'll send him around. You put him straight. If he doesn't, then you tell me and I'll take care of him."

"Do you really think she feeds people she doesn't like laxatives?" North told Mars he didn't want to find out. "Yeah, me either. You tell your dad for me not to take anything from her until he's doing right by her. Even then,

I think I'd hold off. She is a pistol."

Amy was up and around by the time he walked in the door. North held her while she told him of the day she'd had today, as well as the things she'd been working on. Apparently, she was supposed to take a trip to Upper Sandusky, Ohio, to take pictures of the newest member of the animal kingdom, a large nest of breeding American bald eagles. North decided it might be kind of fun to go with her.

Chapter 11

The house was just as neat as she remembered it from her childhood. Charlie sat on the couch that still had stickers on it from when her mom bought it seven years ago. Laughing slightly, she wondered if she could take it back. She wouldn't, of course, but it was funny. Mom not only hadn't gotten around to removing the sales tags, but the pillows to it were sitting in the corner wrapped in plastic.

Cleaning out her mother's condo wasn't hard. She wasn't anyone that saved much. Rarely did she hang pictures or paintings on the wall. Even her kitchen was sparse — one plate, two forks, and a spoon. For as little time as Mom had spent here, that was all she needed. When Charlie came to see her, they usually opted for eating out. Or having pizza. Mom loved pizza.

Taking her laptop to the living room, Charlie went over all the things her mom had set up for her in the event she were to die. While she knew her mom had made all the arrangements for her funeral and burial, it was just too soon for her to be taking care that Mom's wishes were carried out. Looking around while waiting on her file to open up, she spotted the book North had told her about.

"It's a photo album. I don't want it, mind you, but you should go through it. Your mom would cut out things she found in the paper or take pictures of things at work. She would catalog them, then research them later. It was a habit she just couldn't break herself of." Charlie asked North what sort of stuff she found at work. "I know there is a picture of myself in it. When I'd been particularly beaten by one of the servants that worked for my mom. It was an injustice, she told me. For a woman to do this to a grown man. She would take pictures of things left out of their containers that would piss her off. Also, memos made their way into the book that she didn't plan on following. Just things she found annoying or even wrong. It was sort of her own way, I think, of being a rebel. Which we both know she was a trendsetter on some things."

Her mom had been too. She didn't adhere to any rules she didn't understand. Like, why did one have to have breakfast type foods at the first part of the day? Or high heels with a pair of shorts? Charlie loved her mom to pieces and hoped she'd known it. Charlie also hoped she had the same sort of spirit her mom had had.

The knock at the door startled her from her memories. The laptop had long since shut down again. Getting up, she wasn't surprised to see North in the doorway, and he'd brought with him his lovely wife. After introductions were made, they sat around the living room and talked about Lorinda Wessex. It was Amy that asked what the funeral arrangements were.

"None. Not now, anyway. I've donated her body to be used any way they need it. It was what she wanted. Her organs have been harvested and are hopefully bringing someone else as much joy as my mom had in life." Amy told her she was sorry. "Don't be. My mom knew that someday someone might come gunning for her. She knew too that I'd do just what she wanted no matter how much pain it gave me. Pulling the plug for her was the hardest thing I've ever had to do for her, but it was just exactly what she wanted."

"You're very brave." Charlie said she was a bitch, but thanked Amy. "If you don't mind me asking, what are your plans for you? North said she left you this place. You should hang around. Get to know the people that knew her."

"I can't. For as much as I'd like to spend time here with you two, I've got a few things I'm working on back at the university—a few goals I set for myself—one of them being getting my doctorate in nursing. I've been a nurse for the last ten years, working on getting my education high enough where I could run a department at a hospital. But after a while, all I wanted to do was finish up and continue being the best nurse I could be. I think I'm doing it the right way too, by keeping up with my education as well as the things going on around me." North asked her what hospital she worked at. "Mercy General. It's a small hospital, but I do work at the larger one when they're short-staffed. Which I'm thinking is all the time lately."

North helped her pack up her mother's pitiful amount of clothing. Her mother had worn scrubs a great deal, even on her days off, so there was little in the way of dressy things. Why scrubs? she'd asked her mother once. She told her they were nicer looking than sweats, and no one asked her what kind of deal she could get for a family member that fucked up.

The jewelry box Charlie had made for her mom when she was about ten was the only thing on top of her dresser. It was filled with the noodles that had fallen off over the years, and the wedding ring from her marriage to Charlie's dad. He had been murdered one night just after Charlie was born. As far as she knew, her mom hadn't dated much after he was gone.

"This is a really nice condo. I didn't know your cousin owned it until I saw him and his wife walking around yesterday. He even gave me the keys to the shed thing Mom had out back. I haven't had a chance to go out and see what is in there, but I'm betting whatever it is, it's neat as a pen." North said he'd go look for her if she wanted him to. Agreeing with him to do it, Charlie sat back on the couch with Amy, who was helping her go through some of the books her mother had kept.

"They're not really much more than a few smut books,

and a how-to book on making a greenhouse. Did she ever put it up?" Charlie laughed and said the book was from her. She'd gotten it for her mother when she was bitching about working. "You thought she'd enjoy putting in a greenhouse?"

"No. She was thinking if she quit her job, she'd become a hermit. I told her she'd already picked up the habit of eating like one. Hermits, I told her, tended to eat whatever they found in the woods. Since she wasn't keen on foraging for herself, I told her she needed to start growing her own food. We laughed for days about her growing food." Amy laughed with her. "We had some good times, the two of us. We never took much seriously, and if we had to, we did enjoy that too. Mom would have liked you, I think."

"North has told me some about her. I'm not sure I could have done what she did after your dad was killed. To finish up school and then find his murderer must have been a full-time job for her." Charlie said that was her mother in a nutshell. Do or die. "Do you know what happened to her? I mean that my sister is the one that murdered her?"

"Yes. I'm not going to hold anything like that against you, Amy. North told me what happened and how you were related to Phoenix. She and your mother sound like a trip from hell if you ask me." Amy thanked her. "How is that going? Are they going to face some serious jail time?"

"Oh, yes. My mom is the worst kind of person. Not nearly as bad as North's mother was, but almost so. Did you know Eita?" Charlie said that she had, and hated her from the first. "I guess that's the way a great many people felt about her. She had Holly Wilkerson kidnapped, then later murdered. I wonder at times how the boys ended up the way they are."

"Friends. Mostly due to Holly. I knew her, as well. But they had friends that would help them out. Take them in when they needed it. Someone to brush them off, bandage them up if they needed that, and hug them. North and Mars, they were good for each other. Holly kept them safe as much as she could." Amy told her that was what she'd heard. "My mom liked Holly too. I know that sounds lame right now, but I'm thinking the two of them are up there in Heaven, comparing notes on the people that murdered them. I'm so sorry. I just realized what I said."

"Don't be. I'm sure you're right. Holly would be the one she'd go to. I know I would."

Charlie talked to Amy for another half hour. When North appeared, he had cobwebs in his hair as well as a huge tear in his pants. They both asked him what he'd been doing.

"I sort of got myself sidetracked. By the way, there are some boxes in the shed, but nothing in them. Just boxes." Charlie thought that sounded like her mother. "Anyway. After I was finished looking through the boxes, two little boys came up and asked me if I'd help them get their ball from the tree. I haven't any idea how they got that sucker as high as they did, but I nearly broke my neck trying to be all macho by climbing up it. After I braved that, they wanted to play with me. It was great. The kids seemed to have enjoyed it too."

"That would be Rock and Stone Trainer. Twin brothers. I think they're about six or seven now. They're good kids if just a little on the rambunctious side. Mom would bake them cookies when they helped her around the yard. Mostly picking up sticks or something. I think their mom works a great deal to support the three of them." Amy asked about the dad. "I haven't ever seen a man there. Mom said she didn't think he was in the picture much. Mom would hire Shanda when she could to help her around the house."

"That sounds like your mom."

They talked about her mom for the next couple of hours. Amy helped with the files on her mom's computer while North loaded up the things she didn't want to deal with in his truck and took them to the Salvation Army drive. Even Mom's clothes were put in a large box and taken. By nine that night, the condo was not only cleaned up but devoid of any traces of her mom other than the few things she was taking home with her.

"I can't thank you enough for your help. I knew it wouldn't be hard, but you guys being here helped me get through it." North and Amy told her they were glad to have been there for her. "I'm going to leave in the morning to take care of a couple of things for my home, then I'll be back in a week. I have to sign off on some of the benefits Mom left for me."

"If you need me to represent you in any way, you tell

me, Charlie. I loved your mom. She was a good and fair person."

Charlie hugged them both and left the condo when they did. The only thing left to be picked up was the couch, and the man coming for it would be there in the morning. North was going to meet him for her.

Driving back to the hotel, she wondered how to thank the town for the way they'd come together to pray for her mom. Surely there was some sort of fund she could set up for the local high school or something. Charlie thought of how to go about that all the way through getting ready for bed. While she didn't have much in the way of details about what she wanted, she was sure that with the help of North, she could get it set up.

Her cell was ringing when she stepped out of the shower the next morning. It was the hospital. They wanted to know what she wanted them to do with her mom's personal belongings that had come in with her. Not having any idea what that might be, she referred them to North. He'd take care of it for her. Then she called him as soon as she hung up from the hospital.

"I can take care that it's disposed of or brought here for you. I should have suggested that sooner." Charlie said it was fine, but she didn't have time today to deal with it. "Don't worry about it, Charlie. I'll call you if there is a problem. Don't worry about anything here. I have your number, and you have mine. We'll get things taken care of soon enough."

Thankful for such a friend, she was nearly to the airport when she remembered something her mom had told her. North Wilkerson was a man to trust. She knew that to be true, especially after the last few days of him helping her out. Charlie was going to do something nice for him and his new wife. She just had to figure out what it might be.

Sitting on the plane, waiting for their turn in line to take off, it hit her that her mom was gone. Crying a little, she thought of all the things she and her mom had done when she'd been living at home. Even after Charlie had left home, they got together as often as they could.

There was always a story to tell her mom, or Mom had one for her. They spoke to each other every day by phone or by video chat. Charlie was going to miss her so much. Wondering if she'd ever not hurt when she thought of her mom, Charlie decided that the saying, "time heals all wounds," had better be right. She was hurting too much right now to ever think she was going to forget someone as wonderful as her mother.

Getting home, she didn't bother unpacking the few things she'd taken but went to her bedroom to lay down. She was exhausted but more hurting than anything. As she laid there, sobbing out her grief over the death of her mom, Charlie wondered if she'd enjoy living back there where people had known her mom so well. It was something to think about.

~*~

Wats leaned back in his chair and closed his eyes.

He loved being able to work for himself, but he'd been working much too hard. The family alone was keeping him hopping. Thinking of the conversation he'd had with his cousin Shawn today, he wondered what was going to happen to him when he figured out that life could throw you a curveball without any notice.

"I'm going to take some time off." Wats asked him what he was going to do that for. "I'm thinking if I don't get my home in order now, I'm going to be sitting here with an empty house when I'm sixty years old. Not that it's old, but the house is so empty, it's like living in a tomb."

"All right. Not that I think you'd need time off to buy some furniture, but I hope you get it done the way you want it." Shawn told him he was going to fill it with things he loved that he picked up at estate auctions. "Why? I mean, great, but why?"

"When was the last time you were at my parents' home?" Wats said he didn't remember. "Yeah, well, it's all steel and glass. I don't know if Dad even likes it. Anyway, I'm going to get things that speak to me. Dad is going to go on this trip with me. He's thinking he is going to love living in the condo. At least his brothers are close by, and he can walk to town if he wants. We're going to have some fun getting to know each other."

"Now that I can get behind. What is your dad doing with his home?" Uncle Hank hadn't been in his house since Penny had been arrested. They all called her that now, and it was fun. "My dad is going to sell his as soon as he gets it emptied out. It seems none of them were very thrilled about returning to their homes."

"Dad is donating the house to the city. I haven't any idea what they're going to do with it—it's really run-down—but he gave them the property there too. That's about fifty acres. I'm thinking they're going to tear the house down then put in something equally ugly." No doubt. Wats told him about North's dad running for mayor. "He'd be really good at that. With as long as this family has lived here, he'd know just about anything and everything about the town."

Wats sat up when his phone rang. He thought he'd put it on the service, but he might not have gotten it right. There was a learning curve on just about everything he did lately. Saying his name, Wats waited while the person at the other end calmed down enough to speak.

"My grandfather is gone." Wats didn't know what she meant—gone as in missing or gone that he'd died. "He's not here. I came in this morning to stay with him while I finished up my classes, and we had a nice breakfast. Then when I went to the university to see about the classes I would need, I came home, and someone had been in here. There is blood all over the place too."

"Did you call the police?" There was a long pause, and Wats asked her again. "I don't even know who this is or what your grandfather's name is."

"My grandda is James Oliver. My name is Rayne Oliver. Why do you think he had your phone number in his phone marked as police?" Wats said that he didn't have any idea. "I'm going to call the police now. I'm so sorry to have bothered you."

"It's no trouble. I'm on my way there with my medical bag. When we find him, I'll be able to see how he's faring." He didn't want to say anything about him maybe being dead. Lots of blood could be scary enough. "I'm going to call my cousins in too. All of us can look for him."

Wats called the others and told them what was going on. He also mentioned how his number was listed as the emergency number. He called North last, as his number had been busy when he'd called him the first time.

"He's with me at my house." Wats turned his car around and headed toward North's home. "As for the blood, I don't know. There wasn't any there when the two of us left there a few hours ago."

"She said there was a great deal of it." Wats parked in the parking lot of the store he was nearby and tried to catch his breath. "What should I do? Go there and find out what is happening or just go back to my offices?"

"Why don't you go and see if you can talk to Rayne in person? Then perhaps bring her to my house. I don't think she should be driving if she's that upset." Wats told him he'd go out there now. "Be careful, Wats. Since we have no idea what the blood is from, someone might still be in the house."

"Well, thank you very much for that thought."

He made his way to the house carefully. There didn't

seem to be any cars along the way that were parked without anyone in them. Nor did he see any indication of trouble. By the time he was pulling up in front of the house, there were two cruisers there, and a young woman on the front porch rocking in the rocker set out there.

"Your cousin called here. He told me that my grandda was with him." Wats told her he'd take her there if she wanted to go. "I do. I hope you don't mind, but I have to wait on the police. They're doing their thing in there now. I was terrified."

Wats checked her over. He told her he didn't want anything to be wrong with her and checked not just her blood pressure, which was just a little high, but her temperature too. When he was able to give her a clean bill of health, he sat down on the porch in front of her.

"I've known your grandda for a while. When I was in med school, he was one of the free patients that, as students, we were to work with. He's a very healthy man for his age." Rayne told him he didn't sit around on his duff like a lot of people his age. "I think I remember him being about eighty? I could be wrong."

"He'll be ninety-three on his next birthday. Which is coming up. He's all I care about in the world now. My parents are both gone. I don't have any sisters or brothers. No aunts that I want to be around either." She laughed. "The last time I was here, he and his sister, my aunt Carol, had this big to do about him living alone. Christ, he's a few years older than her and looks like he could be her kid.

Not really, but Grandda is in really wonderful shape."

Wats told her about the house that was going to be built for him, and how his cousin, North, was going to make sure he was going to be all right living out here alone. Rayne told him she had planned on living with him until she graduated next year, then she was hoping she could get him to move in with her.

"I've had a little house since my parents died. It's not much, but it's a damned sight better than this is. I guess North, as you called him, saw what he was living in here." Wats told her how he'd only just bought the house a few weeks ago. "The banker that was holding the place didn't want to do anything for him. Told my grandda he'd be better off in a nursing home if he didn't like this place. Grandda lost Grannie here. He doesn't want to leave without going to her, he told me."

By the time the police were finished up with the house, they'd discovered that a raccoon had made its way into the house when it had been attacked by something larger. The blood was all animal blood. It was confirmed it was a raccoon when they found his body in the bedroom that Grandda used.

"I think he's been feeding the poor thing. Grandda is allergic to cats and doesn't care for dogs. They're too big for him to handle, he told me. But this little raccoon made his way into his heart, and he's been taking care of him. I think it was making the loneliness more tolerable." Wats thought that was the nicest thing he'd heard in a while. "I don't know if we'll be able to stay here now. At least not tonight."

"I have a condo you can stay in. I mean by yourself. With your grandda. I'll be someplace else." Wats let out a long breath. "I have a furnished condo the two of you can stay in. I'll bunk with my dad. He's close to where you two can stay."

"I don't want to put you out." Wats assured her she wouldn't be. He was enjoying spending time with his dad. "If you're sure?"

"I am sure. You gather up some things for him to wear, and tomorrow we'll come back here to see what we can salvage out of the bedroom. After that, North is going to take care of getting something more livable in here for the two of you." Wats hoped his dad didn't mind him staying with him a few days. "You get some things, like I said, and I'll make a couple of calls. That way, by the time you're finished here, I can have my arrangements made as well."

As he figured, Dad was happy to have him. North said he was his hero for doing this. All Wats had wanted to do was go to bed and not wake up anytime soon. It was stressful being the worrier of the family. Taking Rayne to his brother's house, then to the condo, was about all he could handle this evening. Going to his dad's condo, Wats was thrilled that he didn't seem to mind him rushing off to bed, and let Wats go without bombarding him with questions.

As soon as his head hit the pillow, Wats knew he wasn't

far from sleep. When a phone rang somewhere in the place, he had to catch himself from getting up and answering it. Being dead tired as he was, he didn't think he could make a sound decision on whether or not he liked chocolate ice cream or vanilla. Or even both for that matter.

Thinking briefly of the list he'd brought from his office, Wats wondered if any of the others would help him out with it. He needed someone to work for him to answer phones. To clean up after him and his patients. Also, Wats needed to get laid.

Laughing a little, he rolled to his side and smiled. Tomorrow was going to be a brand new day, and he was going to try his best not to be running all over town again. Yes, he thought as slumber took him under, tomorrow was a brand new day.

AWARD WINNING, BESTSELLING AUTHOR

Kathi Barton, a winner of the Pinnacle Book Achievement award as well as a best-selling author on Amazon and All Romance books, lives in Nashport, Ohio, with her husband, Paul. When not creating new worlds and romance, Kathi and her husband enjoy camping and going to auctions. She can also be seen at county fairs with her husband, who is an artist and potter.

Her muse, a cross between Jimmy Stewart and Hugh Jackman, brings her stories to life for her readers in a way that has them coming back time and again for more. Her favorite genre is paranormal romance, with a great deal of spice. You can visit Kathi on line and drop her an email if you'd like. She loves hearing from her fans. aaronskiss@gmail.com.

Follow Kathi on her blog: